BODY AT
BUCCANEER'S BAY

DEAD MEN TELL NO TALES

Mystery Bookshop owner Ellery Page
and Police Chief Jack Carson
are diving for the legendary pirate galleon
Blood Red Rose when they discover
an old-fashioned diver's suit,
water-damaged and encrusted with barnacles.

Further examination reveals that
the twentieth century suit contains
a twenty-first century body.

Who was the mysterious diver?
No one seems to be missing
from the quaint and cozy town of Pirate's Cove.
Was the victim really diving for pirate's gold?
And if not, what exactly did he do
to earn that bullet hole in his skull?

BODY AT BUCCANEER'S BAY

SECRETS & SCRABBLE BOOK FIVE

JOSH LANYON

VELLICHOR BOOKS

An imprint of JustJoshin Publishing, Inc.

BODY AT BUCCANEER'S BAY: AN M/M COZY Mystery
(Secrets and Scrabble Book 5)
June 2021
Copyright (c) 2021 by Josh Lanyon
Edited by Keren Reed
Cover and book design by Kevin Burton Smith
All rights reserved.

ISBN: 978-1-945802-77-5
Published in the United States of America

JustJoshin Publishing, Inc.
3053 Rancho Vista Blvd.
Suite 116
Palmdale, CA 93551
www.joshlanyon.com

This is a work of fiction. Any resemblance to persons living or dead is entirely coincidental.

To my much-tried and long-suffering readers. Thank you so much for your patience, your kindness, and your unfailing support.

Sea Shell, Sea Shell,
Sing of the secrets you know so well.

CHAPTER ONE

Gulls circled overhead, mewing plaintively.

Water sloshed and lapped against the side of the rocking boat. The hot, bright August afternoon smelled of diesel and brine and rubber and…liverwurst.

Ellery said, "Hey, do you remember that poison-pen letter I got a while back?"

"Yep." Jack spoke absently, double-checking the regulator and hoses of Ellery's diving equipment.

Jack Carson was Pirate's Cove's police chief and Ellery's boyfriend. He was also a certified diver. Scuba was his one and only hobby, so it was no surprise he owned his gear, but Ellery was renting everything from his flippers to his air tanks, and Jack was not a believer in leaving anything to chance.

"Whatever came of that? Anything? I mean, did the lab find any fingerprints?"

Jack glanced automatically toward the bow of the *Fishful Thinkin'*, where "Cap" Elijah Murphy sat in the cockpit, eating a sandwich and arguing amiably with whoever was at the other end of the ship-to-shore radio. Although technically employed at the *Scuttlebutt Weekly*, Cap was no reporter, let alone a gossip columnist. He contributed a weekly editorial wherein he detailed his fierce objections to any and all changes to Buck Island in general and the village of Pirate's Cove in particular.

"No. That is, the only decipherable fingerprints were yours."

When Ellery didn't respond, Jack squeezed his neoprene-clad shoulder, turning Ellery to face him. "Why? I really think that letter was just..."

"Local hysteria?"

"Well, yeah. Reaction to Trevor's murder."

Ellery's smile was wry. "I thought so too. But."

"But?"

"I got another one yesterday evening."

Jack's blue-green eyes narrowed. "You..."

"Same as before. No stamp. No return address. Heck, no mailing address. Just my name printed on the face of the envelope. Hand-delivered to the Crow's Nest."

"By who? Did you see who dropped it off?"

"No. We were busy all afternoon, and then I let Nora leave at three because we were closing early anyway." Ellery's parents had been arriving on Saturday's five o'clock ferry, and he'd wanted to be there to meet them. They were spending the next week on Buck Island. "I only noticed the letter as I was locking up. It was propped on the base of Rupert's case."

Rupert was a glass-encased resin skeleton clothed in vintage pirate costume, which "greeted" customers as they entered the bookshop. The case was positioned just a few feet from the front door, so someone could easily enter the shop, leave the envelope, and duck out again without ever being seen from the front desk.

Jack's brows formed a single dark, forbidding line. "Did you open it?"

"Of course. It didn't occur to me it was another anonymous letter until I was already reading it."

Jack's scowl deepened. "What did it say? I hope you kept it."

"I kept it."

"Good."

"It was pretty much a repeat performance. *You will die* was the central theme." Ellery said it lightly, but the truth was, he was troubled by the reappearance of his poison-pen pal. Like Jack, he'd dismissed the original anonymous threat as his neighbors' suspicion that he'd murdered Trevor Maples.

If that *wasn't* the reason, what was?

Jack's smile didn't quite reach his eyes, but his tone was brisk, reassuring. "Don't worry about it. We'll find out who this joker is. I promise you they won't be laughing when I'm finished with them."

Ellery nodded. He didn't enjoy receiving anonymous hate mail—who did?—but it wasn't like he was afraid. Back when he'd earned his living playing hapless, haunted Noah Street in the *Happy Halloween!*

You're Dead! movies, he'd received plenty of mail from clearly not-right-in-the-head theatergoers. It kind of went with the job.

Happily, none of the long-distance threats and taunts had ever manifested into a clear and present danger, and he was assuming—hoping—that was the case here.

Still. Not fun.

Jack went swiftly through his own dive prep, testing his regulator, snapping his tank in place on the back of his dive suit, attaching the regulator to the tank, then turning the knob to test the flow of air. He checked his air pressure gauge and appeared satisfied. "Okay. At seventy feet, we'll have about forty minutes down there. Sound good?"

"Sounds great," Ellery said.

"Let's do it."

They clomped their way to the back of the rocking boat.

Before Jack pushed his regulator in his mouth, he warned, "The surge is rougher out here."

"I noticed."

Jack grinned, his teeth white in his tanned face. "Nothing you can't handle."

Ellery grinned back. He appreciated the compliment. He was still new to diving, but he was already hooked.

For their first underwater excursions, Jack had taken him to the Buck Island Pinnacles, a formation of enormous stacked boulders created by the Wisconsin ice sheets eons ago. They'd spent pleasant hours exploring the huge underwater cliffs and swim-throughs, teeming with fish and other ocean life.

Unfortunately, also teeming with tourists.

Now that Jack was satisfied Ellery had the basics down and was as strong a swimmer as he'd claimed, they were venturing farther out, away from the schools of summer visitors, to try diving the numerous wrecks a few miles offshore.

Specifically, they were hunting for the legendary pirate galleon *Blood Red Rose*, reportedly sunk in a hurricane off the island coast in the 1700s. Cap had anchored outside the cove at Seal Point, Buccaneer's Bay, where the *Blood Red Rose* once harbored, safely concealed from the Royal Navy and mainland excisemen. Given that divers had been hunting for the *Blood Red Rose* since the early nineteenth century without luck, Ellery wasn't setting his hopes of pirate treasure too high, though he *was* really looking forward to diving without bumping into charter boats or tourists every few feet.

Jack put his regulator in his mouth, Ellery followed suit, and they rolled backward into the sea.

Oh, that first cold, blue rush.

Blue and then bluer. Cold and then colder. The sudden weightlessness, the feeling of dropping through space and time.

The sudden silence.

Through the stream of bubbles, they signaled *okay* to each other and began releasing air from their vests in preparation for their descent through the shafts of sunlight.

Ten feet down, they sank through a cloud of sleek, silvery-striped fish—a huge school of bass.

It was a little disorienting, that swarming flash and dart of other living creatures—they were the trespassers here—but there was something exhilarating about the encounter too. Ellery reached out, and the fish veered away in synchronized swim. He glanced at Jack and could see Jack's smile around his regulator.

Diving really was about the journey rather than the destination, although no question the destination was always terrific.

The school of bass disappeared as quickly as they'd appeared.

As Jack and Ellery continued down the anchor line, they hit the seasonal thermocline—the transition layer between warmer mixed water at the ocean's surface and cooler deep water below—and with that sudden, startling drop in temperature, came greater visibility, as if a door into another world slid open in invitation.

They continued their descent into silence broken only by the hiss and swallow sounds of their breathing apparatus.

Breathing steadily, normally helped equalize the increasing hydrostatic pressure. Ellery instinctively wiggled his jaw and breathed out through his nose to ease the push against his eardrums.

Jack was right. The current was rougher out here. Nothing Ellery couldn't handle, but yeah, the training wheels were off.

Not far below them were the scattered wrecks, the odd girder sticking up through the swaying green-gold kelp forests, the squat outline of a large boiler, home now to cartoon-colored eelpout, scorpionfish, and crabs.

All was silent but for the bubbles and suction of their regulators.

Jack spotted the massive shape lurking nearby in the water first. He touched Ellery's arm, pointed, and Ellery stared, trying to make out what that huge shadow in suddenly-not-so-distant distance belonged to. Not a shadow. A form. A long, pale form slowly circling them. His breath seemed to freeze in his chest.

Shark.

Not just any shark. He'd seen enough episodes of *Shark Week* to recognize that terrifyingly distinctive shape.

A Great White.

He knew there were sharks in the waters around the island, but he had not been expecting Great Whites. Even as he tried to remind himself that sharks, even Great White sharks, weren't typically aggressive to humans, did not rely on humans for food, and did not—probably—present a genuine threat, he could feel his pulse speeding up, his lungs gulping in more air.

Why the heck was it circling? What did circling mean? Was it getting closer, or was that his alarmed imagination?

This is like a bad movie—and I ought to know.

He jumped as Jack's gloved hand closed on his arm, turned to see where Jack was pointing. He spotted the cavernous skeletal remains of a sunken ship a few yards behind them.

Old but not pirate-ship old. A twentieth century vessel. Some kind of freighter? The hollow structure, starkly black against blue sea, lay tilted on its side, the enormous propellers half buried in the sand.

He could just make out the faded letters of her name: *Roussillon.*

Rigging lines, laden with barnacles, hung from the mast like worry beads, drifting in the current. Coral and sponges transformed the steel hull into aquatic street art, and jewel-bright fish swam through portholes, darting around cables and beams, then doing an about-face and disappearing in an instant like anime fish at the sight of the Great White.

Which was definitely drawing closer.

Definitely.

Ellery could see its eyes now. Black and empty.

Jack didn't have to point twice. Ellery turned and swam for the wreck as strongly and smoothly as he could. And God bless Benjamin Franklin or whoever had invented swim fins.

As Ellery reached the black square void of entrance, he hesitated, afraid the shark would follow them, that they would be trapped inside with a cold-blooded threshing machine, but Jack thumped his shoulder lightly, and Ellery finned into the first compartment.

This was some kind of hold, an area as huge, lightless, and cold as outer space. Ellery's chest felt tight with pressure. Not the hydrostatic kind. The dark. The cold. The unknown. All of it pressed in on him. He had to fight his instinctive resistance. His fear.

And then Jack's flashlight came on, creating a tunnel of light before them, and Ellery's anxiety subsided a little. A turtle flapped across the beam and disappeared.

Jack said something, the words garbled, but his tone—even underwater and laced with bubbles—was ridiculously calm.

Jack had to have dived this wreck before because he was moving without hesitation, guiding the way through an entryway and then down what appeared to be a companionway. Ellery followed, aware of things moving eerily in the shadows, recoiling from the light and motion, retreating.

Their raspy, bubbling breaths bounced noisily off the steel walls.

Good thing he didn't suffer from claustrophobia. Ellery had been in some creepy places, both real life and movie sets, but the bowels of this dead ship were by far the creepiest.

They reached another passageway, empty and dark, and slipped through a doorway far too narrow for a shark the size of the one they'd seen.

How much farther were they going? How much air did they have left?

What if Jack got this wrong?

He didn't want—it wasn't his nature—to obey without question, without hesitation, so why the heck was he blithely swimming through the lightless corridors of this metal tomb? Once again, Ellery had to squelch his rising consternation.

And then they were swimming upward in the flooded compartment, popping to the inky surface like a pair of corks. Jack pulled off his mouthpiece.

Ellery followed suit, pulled out his own regulator with shaking hands, gasping.

"Holy—"

A small pocket of air, at least partly comprised of their own exhaled bubbles, had collected against the ceiling.

"We're okay here." Jack's voice echoed weirdly in the compartment. "We'll give our friend a little space."

"Was that what I thought it was? That wasn't like a-a thresher shark, right?"

"No. It looked like—it wasn't a thresher." Jack looked and sounded calm, but then Jack would do his best to look and sound calm in the worst circumstances.

"Yikes."

"Yeah."

"How long are we—can we—hang out here?"

"We're okay. We should have almost fifteen minutes before we've got to start back."

Ellery nodded. Fifteen minutes was a long time underwater, but not so long when you were hoping to outwait a shark.

Jack said, "Let's check your gauge."

Ellery offered a look at his console. He was fully capable of checking his own gauge, but in this, he trusted Jack's judgment above his own.

Yes. He trusted Jack in a way he couldn't re-member trusting anyone before. Anyone who wasn't already family. Certainly, he would never have trust-ed Brandon with his life. Or wallet. Nor even Todd. That had to mean something, right?

Jack grunted. "Maybe more like ten minutes."

"I know. I'm using up my air too fast. That shark—why was it circling us?"

"Trying to figure out what we were, most likely."

"Because in movies—"

"In real life they usually attack from below."

"Okay," Ellery said doubtfully.

Jack winked. "We should probably save our breath." He was not really a winky kind of guy, so he was trying to reassure Ellery. Ellery would have been more reassured if he hadn't realized Jack was *trying* to be reassuring, but he appreciated the effort.

He was hoping with all his heart the shark was gone by the time they left the ship. That thing had been eight feet long at least. *At least.* The very thought of it made him feel queasy. Until now, he hadn't realized he was afraid of sharks. Theater critics, spiders, financial ruin, sure. But a Great White put the hairiest of spiders—and theater critics—into a whole different perspective.

They waited, treading water, their clammy breaths bouncing off the claustrophobically low ceiling.

"That ought to do it." The metallic reverberation of Jack's voice jolted Ellery from his uneasy reflections.

"You think?" That had to have been the fastest ten minutes on record.

Jack nodded, said firmly, "See you topside."

Regulator in place, Jack sank slowly beneath the surface, bubbles popping on the slick water.

Ellery pushed his regulator back in, felt the sweet stream of oxygen, and submerged, trying not to think about whether the shark would be waiting for them when they left the wreck. Probably not. A shark that size probably had his priorities straight. Probably knew better than to waste time on a pair of funny-tasting seals.

His eyes adjusted to the unexpected brightness of Jack's flashlight beam cutting a swath through the murky water. Jack headed for the doorway in a couple of strong kicks.

Ellery followed, but something—the suggestion of motion in the water behind him—made him glance back, then do a double take. The good news was, the shark had not somehow sneaked inside the compartment. The bad news... Well, it wasn't *bad* news, but what the heck was it?

He peered through the cloudy water, trying to understand what he was seeing, trying to make sense of that strange misshapen brown form drifting on an invisible current.

That weird bulbous head like a...like a space alien staring straight at him.

Horror washed through him as suddenly, belatedly, he realized what he was seeing.

Another diver.

He yelled on a stream of bubbles, and Jack, who had slipped through the entrance, shot back inside the compartment as Ellery clambered back to the surface.

Ellery tore his regulator out of his mouth, gasping the too thin air, mostly carbon dioxide at this point. "Holy freaking...moly!"

Jack yanked his mouthpiece out. "What? What is it?"

"There's something, someone, down there! A-a diver."

"A *diver*?" Jack sounded confused, instinctively peering down, trying to see through the turbid pool.

"Maybe? I don't know what the hell it was." That was the truth. It had *looked* like a turn-of-the-century diver. A ghost diver. And in this strange underwater world, he could about believe it had been just that. A ghost.

Jack peered at him in the gloom, then without a word, jammed in his regulator and dived down, brushing past Ellery's legs as he directed the flashlight beam around the flooded interior.

Doubtfully, Ellery watched the pallid flicker of light, probing here and there, dissolving into darkness. Had he imagined that vision straight out of *20,000 Leagues Under the Sea*?

But no. He hadn't. Jack was back in seconds, gloved hand clenched on a fistful of what looked like brown canvas.

An old diving suit.

Jack spat the regulator out, said, "We'll talk surface side. Time to go. Now." He jammed the regulator back in and descended, heading once more for the compartment entrance.

Ellery pushed his mouthpiece in and followed.

The yellow triangle of Jack's flashlight beam illuminated cross braces and fallen beams as he propelled himself in strong kicks down the passage, dragging the diving suit behind him. Ellery finned after.

The heavy brass helmet bobbed up and down as though nodding encouragement.

"**Y**ou boys took your time," Cap called over the smack and slosh of waves against the hull of the *Fishful Thinkin'*. "Was starting to think you ran into trouble." He reached down to take Ellery's weights and then his vest and tank.

"No trouble," Jack called.

"No? When I saw that fin out there, I started to wonder."

Ellery muttered, "You and me both."

Getting back on the boat was probably the hardest part of diving. Conscious of Jack patiently treading water a safe distance behind him, Ellery gripped the handrail of the boat ladder and removed his fins, one at a time, before stepping onto the ladder rung and scrambling aboard.

He pulled his mask off. As much as he enjoyed diving, there was no better feeling than the roll of deck beneath his feet, those first deep breaths of fresh air, the kiss of sunlight on his face. All of it felt especially wonderful today.

"That shark was a Great White," he told Cap.

"Was it? Well, they're out there whether we see 'em or not." Cap leaned over the gunwale to take Jack's weight belt. "What have you got there?"

"Ellery found an old diving suit." Jack handed over his BCD and tank, and then hauled the heavy diving suit up.

"More like, it found me." Ellery joined Cap in grabbing for the canvas suit, which snagged on the ladder with an alarming tearing sound.

"What in tarnation? Sure the diver isn't still in it? This thing weighs a ton."

"Hold on." Jack awkwardly shifted his grip on the ladder. "Take the helmet first."

The barnacle-encrusted, pig-snout copper helmet appeared welded to the corselet, which was firmly clamped to the water-stained twill, so Ellery and Cap had to haul the suit by the bonnet up the ladder while Jack pushed and bunched from below. The helmet banged against the railing, the collection bag thumped against the steps as though filled with chains. Finally, they managed to dump the stained suit on the deck, the boots landing splayed, the helmet clanging down like the final toll of a bell.

Jack threw his fins over the gunwale, climbed the ladder, and clambered over the side to join Ellery and Cap. They stared down at the crumpled suit.

In the water, the suit had seemed to move with a semblance of ghostly life, but now it lay motionless in a lumpy, rotting pile on the deck of the *Fishful Thinkin'*.

Still, a very cool find.

And yet… Something about the sight of that suit gave Ellery a peculiar feeling in the pit of his stomach. He almost wished he hadn't seen it drifting there, staring at him, like it had been waiting for them.

"Nora's going to be thrilled," Cap remarked. "Where'd you say you found it?"

Jack's mask had left red indentations, making forbidding lines in his face. He was still breathing hard from the effort to get the suit on board.

"We were on the *Roussillon*. What's left of her."

"The *Roussillon*?" Cap's bristling brows rose. "That's funny."

"Why's that?"

"The *Roussillon* sank in 1956. This looks more like 1930s standard diving dress."

Ellery and Jack exchanged looks.

"Maybe they were still using the old suits into the '50s?" Ellery suggested.

"That sounds about right." Cap shrugged. "And I could be wrong about the suit's age. Though it seems to me the Historical Society has a similar one. Maybe a little older. Nora's the one to ask. She'll know."

No question about that. Nora Sweeny, Ellery's assistant—no, now *assistant manager*—at the Crow's Nest bookstore, knew pretty much everything there was to know about Buck Island, past, present, and possibly future.

Ellery was thinking about that, thinking Nora was certain to be delighted with their discovery, as he studied the knobbly, water-stained pile of canvas. He wondered why *he* didn't feel delighted, because it was kind of an amazing find.

But something about this felt…

Wrong.

Worrying.

He asked slowly, uneasily, "Why would the helmet be fastened to the suit?" He could feel Jack and Cap staring at him. "They wouldn't store the diving suit with the helmet already clamped on, would they?"

"No. I guess not," Cap said. He looked at Jack. "He's right."

Ellery was thinking out loud. "But then, if the suit wasn't in storage…"

Jack had to have had the same thought because his, "*Oh hell*," was both dismayed and heartfelt. He squatted down, and using his diving knife, tried to pry open the helmet's rusted and grimy front viewport.

It took some doing, but at last the brass grille and face plate swung to the side, revealing the dark, empty interior of the helmet.

Ellery expelled a breath he hadn't realized he was holding until that moment of relief.

Jack shoved his hair out of his eyes, scooted around so that he could better peer through the helmet into the suit. After a moment, he groaned and rocked back on his heels.

He began to swear.

"No way," Ellery protested. "It *can't* be."

Cap looked in bewilderment from Jack to Ellery. His eyes widened. "You don't mean—You're not saying— Is there someone in there?"

"There was." Jack sounded bitter.

Reluctantly, Ellery maneuvered for a better view—*better view* being a matter of opinion—and at last was able to make out the grisly rictus grin of a skull. Minus all the soft tissue, the body inside the suit had shrunk considerably. Or maybe the diver hadn't been all that big to begin with.

Ellery said faintly, "You're kidding me."

The skull laughed silently back at him.

"Cap, phone the Coast Guard." Jack gazed up at Ellery, his expression pained. He shook his head. "I don't believe it. I think we just swam right through a crime scene."

CHAPTER TWO

"Wait a minute," Talia Alexander (yes, *that* Talia Alexander) interrupted. "What happened to the Great White shark?"

It was Sunday evening, and Ellery was having dinner with his mother (the aforementioned Talia Alexander) and his stepfather, George (the indie director George Alexander), at the Salty Dog pub, which, as usual during the summer months in Pirate's Cove, was packed. They'd been waiting nearly fifteen minutes for a flushed and perspiring Libby Tulley to deliver their second round of drinks.

The plan had been for Jack to join them, but when Ellery had left the marina, Jack had still been on the phone with the Rhode Island State Police, so it was looking more likely with every minute that the official Meet the Parents would have to wait.

"The shark was gone when we left the *Roussillon*. The *shark* isn't the story."

Talia's brown eyes widened. "I think my only offspring nearly being eaten by a shark is most definitely the climax of this narrative."

Ellery rolled his eyes, turned for support to George. George chuckled and shook his head, which was what he usually did when asked to take sides between his two favorite people on the planet. He was a short, stocky man with gray hair and gray eyes. He did not look like a film director or like someone who would be married to Talia Alexander, but he was, and he excelled at both.

He said mildly, "Darling, Ellery's trying to tell us he's involved in a murder case. *Another* murder case."

The previous evening, Tom Tulley, owner and proprietor of the Salty Dog, had seemed to take unreasonable pleasure in regaling Ellery's parents with tales of Ellery's "sleuthing." Talia and George had absorbed this news with a few alarmed glances at each other.

Ellery said quickly, "Me? No, definitely not. I'm definitely not involved in this. I mean, other than bumping into the, er, body."

"It can't be murder," Talia protested. "It must be some kind of-of freak accident. Right?"

"Wrong," George said. "It has to be murder. How else would a skeleton wind up in an antique diving suit at the bottom of a sunken ship?"

"It might not have been an antique diving suit when the victim climbed into it." Ellery had performed some Google-fu while waiting at the bar for his parents. "It turns out that diving suits from the 1930s were still in use in the 1950s. Also, some of the diving suits from the 1950s look a lot like the diving suits from the 1930s, so it's really going to take an expert to figure that piece out."

Probably an expert by the name of Nora Sweeny, although Jack had mentioned plans to contact the Rhode Island Marine Archaeology Project in Newport.

"Even if your skeleton is from the 1950s, what was he doing fully suited up when that ship went down?"

Yeah, that was definitely a problem. Especially since the diver had not been carrying tanks.

"Darling, you sound like you *want* this to be a murder." Talia seemed ever so slightly exasperated.

"Could make a terrific documentary."

Talia opened her mouth—but then her expression grew thoughtful. "*Oh.* I see what you mean."

Ellery could see what George meant too. He could also imagine what Jack would have to say. Assuming this little maritime mystery did turn out to be murder. Which hopefully it would not.

From overhead, a teasing voice said, "At it again, Professor Plum?"

Dylan Carter scrunched up against their table to make way for Libby, who was trying to squeeze past with a precariously balanced tray of beer mugs.

"Hey there." Ellery also had to raise his voice. It was getting louder by the minute inside the pub, and the band hadn't even started yet. Then Dylan's words registered. "Oh no. Don't tell me the news has already reached the village."

Dylan spluttered, "*Already* reached the village? How long did you think it would take? All of Pirate's Cove was speculating on the diver's identity before the *Fishful Thinkin'* even docked."

"Really? Who's the leading contender?"

Dylan laughed. "You'll want to consult the Silver Sleuths on that one." He beamed at Talia and George. "You must be Ellery's parents. What a pleasure to meet you. I'm Dylan Carter. I own the Toy Chest, the little shop next to Ellery's."

Dylan, a slim, silver, effortlessly dapper sixty-something, was one of Ellery's closest friends in Pirate's Cove. At one time, he had been Ellery's *only* friend. There's just something about being suspected of murder that makes people roll up the welcome mat and lock the door. Happily, that was all in the past, and Ellery was now a respected member of the community. Or at least as respected as someone who kept stumbling over murders could be.

Ellery made the introductions. Dylan kissed Talia's hand, shook George's, and accepted the invitation to take the seat Ellery had been saving for Jack.

"Only you could go scuba diving and stumble across a sixty-five-year-old cold case," he told Ellery.

Ellery protested, "Why is everyone so sure this is murder?"

As if he didn't know. But Dylan had raised another puzzling aspect: if that diving suit had been floating around that wreck for almost seventy years, how was it that no other diver had come across it?

"Uh, you live in Pirate's Cove, right? That quaint New England village with a homicide rate second only to Cabot's Cove?"

Talia and George exchanged looks, and Ellery said quickly, "Really. It's not like that at all. I mean, half the village doesn't lock their doors at night."

Dylan intoned, "For which many pay a terrible price."

"Not helping."

"I'm joking, of course. This village is as safe as...as houses."

"*Exactly,*" Ellery said.

"Although, I have to say, ever since you arrived—" Dylan broke off at the look Ellery gave him, and cleared his throat. "So what do you think of our little burg?"

"It's a long way from New York," Talia said. "Have you always lived in Pirate's Cove, Dylan?"

"No, no. I'm a recent transplant, at least by Buck Island standards. In another decade or so, the locals should stop referring to me as *that new feller.*"

"That *other* new feller," Ellery put in.

Dylan chuckled. "That's right. The not-as-new-as-the-*other* new feller." Dylan, being his usual effortlessly charming self, suddenly broke character and said to Talia, "I hope I'm not overstepping, but has anyone ever told you—"

"No," Ellery told him.

"Around the eyes, I think," Talia said. "Maybe the mouth?"

"Oh, definitely the mouth," George murmured.

Dylan gulped, "Wait. You mean? You *are*. Aren't you?"

Well, that was inevitable. In addition to owning the Toy Chest and several other businesses in town, Dylan managed the Scallywags, Pirate's Cove's local theater guild, *and* he was a total movie nut. It was over their shared love of strong cocktails and terrible B-movies that Ellery and Dylan had first bonded.

"I'm right! You're Talia Alexander. This is fantastic. I *adore* your work," Dylan told her.

Ellery and George shared resigned smiles. Talia beamed. Despite a pretty respectable filmography, she got a lot more puzzled *wait-have-we-mets* than requests for autographs.

Dylan threw Ellery a look of reproach. "You didn't tell me your mother was Talia Alexander. You said she taught drama to high-schoolers."

"She does."

"I do," Talia said. "And occasionally I make movies. Mostly to amuse my husband."

Dylan turned to George, said reverently, "George Alexander. Of course. How did I miss that connection? The director of *Little Pitchers*."

George said admiringly, "You sure know your obscure indie box-office disasters."

"It's one of my all-time favorite films."

Further conversation was interrupted as Libby arrived at last with their drinks. In an effort to save time and aggravation—their own, if not Libby's—they had ordered a double round, and the dispensing of glasses (followed by redistribution and subsequent mopping) took a couple of minutes.

Ellery smiled at Libby. "Is this it? Your last night?"

Libby and Felix, both members of the Scallywags, were leaving for college on the mainland, which was definitely going to leave Dylan short a couple of cast members for his next few productions. Felix had also been working at the Crow's Nest. In fact, that day had been his last.

Libby nodded and smiled, though she looked doubtful glancing around the boisterous gathering. "I don't know how Pop's going to manage."

"He'll be fine," Dylan said heartlessly. "I'm the one you should feel sorry for. What am I going to do without my favorite leading lady?"

Libby laughed that off.

Ellery said, "Speaking of leading ladies, where's September?"

September St. Simmons was Dylan's girlfriend, the latest in a very long line of local lovelies.

"Headache," Dylan said briefly.

"Ah."

"Does everyone know what they want?" Libby interrupted hopefully.

Ellery and then Dylan ordered their meals, and Libby turned to George and at last Talia. Talia began the lengthy process of questioning how every dish was prepared, followed by requesting substitutions. George smiled apologetically to no one in particular, and sipped his drink.

As Talia mused the viability of substituting broccoli for noodles in the Corsair's (a.k.a. hamburger) casserole, Dylan continued to gaze soulfully across the table. He murmured, "If your mother was single, I'd marry her in a heartbeat."

"That would be awkward," Ellery said. "Stay away from my mother."

Dylan smirked. "Don't think it's the first time I've heard that one."

Ellery snorted.

A waft of ocean-scented breeze rolled through the room as the pub door swung open. Jack stepped inside—or tried to step inside. The main room was so crowded, he had to scan the floor from the doorway.

Ellery raised his arm, and Jack spotted him. He nodded, and proceeded to work his way along the wall, stopping to talk every few feet with his increasingly inebriated constituents.

Ellery's heart lightened. He really hadn't thought there was any chance of Jack making it to dinner. Not only had Jack made it, he'd taken time to shower and change out of his uniform. Casual blue jeans and white polo shirt really suited his ruggedly handsome looks. His sun-streaked brown hair was still damp from the shower. His blue-green eyes were piercingly bright in his tanned face as he threw Ellery a quick, harassed smile.

Ellery wasn't the only one happy to see Jack. As he watched Jack navigate the shoals of chairs, beach bags, and speeding waitstaff, he noticed a fair-haired man at the packed bar spot Jack, do a double take, and push back his stool in order to intercept him.

"*Jack?*"

Jack turned, so Ellery didn't see his expression—nor could he hear Jack's response—but he was good at reading body language, and the set of Jack's shoulders, the stiffness of his spine, indicated surprise, confusion, then wariness.

Which was…interesting.

More interesting, and revealing, was the other man's face. He seemed equally surprised and confused, but definitely delighted.

Ellery was not insecure or jealous, although having your live-in boyfriend cheat on you with your then best friend did make you a little more…alert to the behavior of people you felt invested in. He felt a ripple of curiosity at just *how* delighted that guy was to see Jack—and how *not* delighted Jack was to see him.

"Who's that?"

Dylan followed Ellery's gaze. He looked surprised. "Blimey. I think that's Rowdy Wallace."

Rowdy Wallace, tall, blond, broad-shouldered, and, in white jeans and navy polo shirt, almost the perfect photo negative to Jack, was speaking eagerly and pointing to the bar. Jack's shoulders had relaxed, his stance was easy, but he was shaking his head. He thumbed over his shoulder in the direction of Ellery's group's table.

"What kind of name is Rowdy?"

"A nickname earned through blood, sweat, tears, and other soggy activities."

"Yikes. Speaking of which."

Dylan winked. "Colby Wallace, a.k.a. Rowdy, was and probably is the black sheep of the family. He's the middle kid. Well, clearly not a kid anymore. None of us are. Present company excepted."

Ellery was thirty-two—thirty-three in October—so he was hardly a kid. "Ha. And who are the Wallaces when they're at home?"

"When they're at home, who knows? Here, they're just rich summer folk." Dylan's tone was dismissive, although the Scallywags Theater Guild depended heavily on the generosity of its rich summer folk patrons.

Ellery said lightly, "Well, there's plenty of that going around this island."

"There is indeed." Dylan continued to study Jack and Rowdy. "I wonder if it's just Rowdy, or whether the whole clan has returned. It's been a long time."

"What's been a long time?"

"Since the Wallaces were *in residence*. Not a one of them have been back in years. Not since the old man drowned. I wonder if they're here for the regatta. *That* would make for an interesting week."

The following day would kick off Buck Island Race Week. Six days of boating activities both on and off the water. This would be Ellery's first race week. From what he'd heard, participants would spend the days racing around the island, wiping out buoys and terrorizing swimmers, and the nights bar-hopping from yacht to yacht. It didn't sound particularly good for business. His own or Jack's.

To Rowdy Wallace's evident disappointment, Jack was already moving away, once more heading toward their table. There was nothing to read on Jack's face, but Rowdy's expression spoke volumes. Ellery couldn't help a final question. "Were Jack and Rowdy close?"

Dylan looked taken aback. "Jack and Rowdy? That all happened years before Jack ever arrived in Pirate's Cove."

Okay. But regardless of whatever had happened years before Jack came to Pirate's Cove, it was pretty clear to Ellery that Jack and Rowdy Wallace *were* previously acquainted.

By then Jack had reached them. Ellery rose. "Hey, you made it!"

Jack's rueful smile acknowledged it had been close. All he said was, "Of course."

Ellery hesitated. He wasn't exactly sure what the protocol was; Jack did not go in for PDAs. But Jack surprised him with a quick, casual kiss. "I wouldn't miss it." His light gaze held Ellery's for a moment, and Ellery's heart warmed.

He turned and made the introductions, and Jack smiled, shook hands, and said all the right things, doing his best to pass the audition. Whether he succeeded had yet to be determined. Ellery knew from long experience his parents could be a tough audience, but the fact that Jack was nothing like any of Ellery's previous boyfriends had to be a point in his favor.

As they were short a chair, Dylan offered to give up his place, but Jack brushed that off, and sure enough, a chair seemed to magically appear from behind the bar. Never being without a place to sit was apparently one of the perks of being the chief of police.

As eager as Ellery was to hear how things had gone with the state troopers, he knew that conversation would have to wait until he and Jack were alone. He'd forgotten to send the memo to his parents and Dylan however, and they began to grill Jack about the body at Buccaneer's Bay.

Jack gave Ellery a pained look, and Dylan said, "Don't blame him. The cat was out of the bag the minute that ambulance drove through the village with its siren blaring and lights flashing on its way to the med center."

Jack winced. "Anyway, you know as much as I do."

"*Clearly* not true," Dylan said to Ellery.

Clearly not, but Ellery refrained from comment.

Libby reappeared to deliver Dylan's martini and take Jack's order. It seemed she had decided to let bygones be bygones because she smiled self-consciously and nodded when Jack asked if tomorrow was the big day.

"We're taking the eleven o'clock ferry."

After Libby moved off, Ellery made an effort to redirect the conversation to island activities his parents might enjoy, but Talia rejected his suggestions of renting mopeds or touring the lighthouse in favor of interrogating Jack.

"Tom Tulley was telling us last night about Ellery's involvement in a couple of your criminal investigations, Jack. How do you feel about that?"

Ellery said, "*I* feel Tom should keep his mouth shut."

"*You* shush. I want to hear what Jack has to say."

Jack's smile was a little wry. "I'm not sure how I feel. It's not something I've run into before with someone I'm seeing."

Talia's brows arched. She looked from Jack to Ellery. "Then you *are* seeing each other?"

"No, no," Ellery said. "It's a custom on the island for the police chief to greet citizens with a kiss."

"Smart-ass."

Jack looked confused. He glanced at Ellery. "Was it supposed to be a secret?"

"Heck no." Ellery said to Talia, "Did I not tell you I wanted you to meet someone?"

"You did. Yes. I assumed you meant Dylan."

Dylan choked on his martini.

Talia said to Jack, "It's just that Ellery's always a little...cagey about his relationships."

"Oh?" Jack's brows drew together. "I see."

Ellery nudged Jack's knee with his own. "No, you don't." To his mother, he said, "You're enjoying this way too much."

"In fairness—"

"In fairness, you referred to Brandon as Young Dracula the whole time we were together."

Talia tilted her head, her expression innocent. "Was I wrong? There are all kinds of bloodsuckers." She added, "You were living with Todd for three months before we ever knew about it."

George said, "Darling, Jack doesn't know you're teasing."

"*Am* I teasing?"

"Yes." George was firm. He repeated to Jack, "*Yes.*"

Ellery shook his head at Jack. This time Jack came to his rescue, saying smoothly, "But in answer to your question, Mrs. Alexander, Ellery's great at figuring out puzzles. He's been...very helpful."

"Now *that* I believe," Talia said. "He's terrific at puzzles. Which makes sense, given that *he's* a puzzle."

Ellery opened his mouth, but this time Jack nudged him, and he subsided.

Thankfully, the band finished setting up and launched into their first number of the evening, a rousing version of "Jack Was Every Inch a Sailor." The music made any meaningful conversation pretty much impossible. Before long, the entire bar was accompanying The Fish and Chippies with a rousing chorus.

> *Jack was every inch a sailor*
> *Five and twenty years a whaler*
> *Jack was every inch a sailor*
> *He was born upon the bright, blue sea*

Ellery met Jack's gaze, dropped his eyelid to half-mast and held it for a meaningful beat. Jack's mouth quirked. He rubbed his ankle suggestively against Ellery's.

Talia glanced at George and smiled into her Drambuie cider cooler.

Another gust of salt-scented night air wafted across the room as the pub door swung open. Jack glanced automatically toward the entrance. There was something in his expression… Ellery followed Jack's troubled gaze in time to see Rowdy Wallace disappear into the night.

CHAPTER THREE

"**O**rdinarily a dive team would make a thorough examination of the area before the body was removed to the surface."

It was nearly midnight by the time Jack and Ellery finally arrived home. Dinner had been followed by a stroll with George and Talia down to the harbor to watch the moonlight on the water, and then it had been back to the Salty Dog for a final round of drinks before Talia and George had retired to their upstairs suite. After that, Ellery had stopped to pick up Watson from his puppysitter before following Jack to Captain's Seat.

A long and eventful day. An exhausting day. Ellery wanted nothing more than to close his eyes and fall asleep to the night lullaby of rustling maple leaves and chirping crickets, but Jack was keyed up, speaking over the splashing of the bathroom sink as he readied for bed. Hopefully for bed. Hopefully Jack was not working himself up to driving back to Pirate's Cove and burning some midnight oil.

Ellery called back, "Would it really have made that much difference? How much of an examination could be done underwater?" He hated to see Jack beat himself up over something he had no way of knowing or preventing.

Jack poked his head out of the bathroom, pointing his toothbrush for emphasis. "There are all kinds of things that should and would be done, same as on land: taking photos and sketches of the crime scene, taking measurements, taking compass readings."

"Ah. Right."

"The body itself. Hands, feet, and head are supposed to be bagged. Then the remains are placed in a body bag with mesh panels for water drainage."

Not a pleasant image on which to head off to dreamland, but this was the reality of dating a cop. A cop who believed it was on him to keep everyone safe and their little island secure.

"Okay, but, Jack, there's a good chance this guy died back in the 1950s, trying to salvage the *Roussillon* after it went down."

"It's possible." Jack's tone was far from convinced.

"It's not just possible. It's the most probable answer, right? I mean, what's the alternative?"

Jack shook his head. "I don't like the fact that he—or she—didn't have tanks or hoses or a dive line."

She? Was that a possibility? Probably not if the diver had indeed died circa 1950.

"I can't explain the tanks, but maybe the hoses and dive line deteriorated. It's been over sixty years. It's not like the ship was preserved in ideal conditions."

"Agreed. But." Jack said what Ellery was privately thinking, "*Something* ought to be left. Rubber can last decades in seawater."

Yeah. No air hose? No lines of any kind? It was troubling for sure. Since moving to Pirate's Cove, Ellery had seen plenty of drawings and paintings and photos of old-timey mariners. Divers of that era were always coiled in ropes and hoses as if being swallowed by sea snakes. Something surely would have been left of those hoses and lines.

Jack added, "And he should still have his tanks."

Right. Those damned tanks. Twin tanks back then. Under what circumstances would a diver not bother with air tanks, air hose, or diving line?

Circumstances in which the diver did not plan to return to the surface.

Or circumstances in which someone else did not plan for the diver to return to the surface.

Jack disappeared into the bathroom once more, leaving Ellery with his thoughts. Which, despite the grisly discovery of that afternoon, were mostly pleasant. He had enjoyed dinner. It was great seeing his parents again. And he was very happy that Jack had made the effort to be there. Not just physically there, but mentally and emotionally there. However worried Jack might be about this new cold—and wet—case, he had been alert, attentive, and even charming in his quiet, serious way. Sure, it had been plain from the outset that unlike Todd (or even Dylan), he had never heard of Ellery's parents and had no knowledge of the film industry. Heck, Jack had never even seen one of Ellery's movies. And that was fine with Ellery. All of it. Frankly, it was kind of refreshing.

He smiled faintly, contemplating the black puddle of Watson snoring softly between his feet. The sweet, summery smell of the meadow floated through the open window. The pale face of the August moon peered through the whispering maple leaves into the master bedroom. Moody shadows played over the life-sized portrait of his famed pirate-hunting ancestor Captain Horatio Page.

Legend had it, the captain had died at the ripe old age of 102 in this very bed. Alone. History that Ellery had no intention of repeating.

The sink taps turned off. Jack snapped out the bathroom light and padded into the bedroom.

Watson's tail stirred, but he didn't open his eyes. Ellery's eyes were open, though. Head comfortably propped on his arms, he admired the picture presented by Jack, lean, tanned, and muscular, in his immaculate, white skivvies. He couldn't help noticing that Jack's expression, as he climbed into bed, remained preoccupied.

Ellery sighed mentally and refocused his thoughts. "Okay, if it wasn't a diving accident, what do you think happened?"

Jack's smile was sardonic. "You, of all people, are asking me what could possibly have happened?"

"Murder?" Ellery was not surprised. He'd been trying to convince himself all evening he was reading evil intent into a tragic accident, but there were just too many red flags.

Jack thumped his pillows into shape against the headboard, and relaxed into the stack. "It's one possibility. There are others."

"Are there? But seriously. Can you think of an alternative explanation?"

"Sure. Someone dressed up for Buccaneer's Day, got drunk, thought it would be funny or cool to try wreck-diving in historical costume, got trapped on the *Roussillon*, and ultimately drowned."

Ellery's jaw dropped. "It's startling how fast you came up with that. Would that be typical Buccaneer's Day behavior?"

"Nope. And it wasn't fast. I've been running possible scenarios all afternoon. The problem with this particular theory is someone would surely have noticed our Buccaneer's Day victim was missing."

"What if he was on his own?" Not that it seemed very likely. Where was the fun in attending a big drunken brawl all by yourself?

"Even if he'd gone diving alone, his boat would have been anchored in the bay, which would have led to obvious conclusions. There would surely have been an investigation."

Sure as hell on Jack's watch.

"Right." Ellery mulled that over for a moment or two. "Not only that. Where would he come up with historical diving gear? Because that didn't look like a costume to me. Not that I'm an expert in standard diving dress, but I'm an expert in costumes, and the kind of thing you can buy off the rack isn't usually *that* detailed. That suit looked authentic, right down to the collection bag and boots."

"It did," Jack agreed. "It looked like the real thing to me."

"Those suits aren't just lying around. If someone loaned that out, they'd want it back. A suit like that in good condition would probably be worth a lot of money."

"That's a good point," Jack said thoughtfully. He smiled suddenly, quizzically. "Why aren't your parents staying with you?"

"Oh." Ellery glanced at Watson. "George is allergic to dogs."

"Oh no."

Watson let out a long and disconcertingly human-sounding moan.

Jack and Ellery exchanged grins.

"I swear he understands what we're saying," Ellery said.

"If you get any blackmail letters, you'll know who's behind it."

Ugh. Ellery had forgotten about the anonymous threat he'd received. Some of his contentment faded.

It was unsettling to think that one of his neighbors felt such hostility toward him. Why?

He pushed his unease aside. "Also, if my mother was staying here for more than a day or two, she'd end up clearing out the attic or something. She's not good at sitting still. She likes to be where the action is."

Jack quirked an eyebrow. "Yeah? I can see that. Your mom's a pistol."

"Unregistered and fully loaded." But Ellery was smiling. He loved his mother to pieces. He loved having the chance to show her around Pirate's Cove, the chance to introduce her to the new people in his life. That said, she could be a little overwhelming. He was glad Jack was not the easily overwhelmed type. "I'm just glad we were able to talk her out of ordering that second round of shots."

Jack concurred. "How'd you get them a room at the Salty Dog on such short notice? Tom told me they've been booked up since May."

Ellery said grimly, "Libby owed me a favor."

"*Ah*. Right."

"Anyway, it's only for two nights. Tomorrow they check into the Seacrest Inn."

"They'll like that. The evenings are a lot quieter, the food is terrific, and Nan's a sweetheart."

"Yeah."

"George seems like a nice guy."

"George *is* a very nice guy." Ellery added, "I'm sorry the conversation got stuck on movies and movie-making and theater and…theatrics."

"What?" Jack looked surprised. "I thought it was interesting. Dylan's part of that world, you're part of that world. It's natural you're going to talk shop. It was just the same when I was in LAPD."

"You and the other detectives used to sit around talking box-office returns?"

"It was California." But then Jack was serious. "I mean it. I had a good time. Your mom's a hoot, and I think there's a lot of George in you, even if he is your stepdad."

"I like that idea. I love them both."

Jack's smile crinkled the corners of his eyes in a way that always gave Ellery a sort of sunshiny feeling in his chest. "I can tell."

"I've been so busy these last months, I didn't realize how much I missed them."

Jack said after a moment, "It's mutual. I think your mom really wants you to come back to New York."

Ellery shrugged. "She does. But."

"But?"

"I don't see that for myself. I'm happy in Pirate's Cove. I feel at home here. I know it probably sounds odd because I've only lived here a few months, but I feel like I belong."

"You do belong."

They smiled into each other's eyes.

Ellery reached up and turned out the lamp.

"**A**nother thing. I've dived that site before. I can't understand how I never came across that diving suit."

On the verge of sleep, Ellery jerked back to wakefulness. The moon had slipped down the sky, and the room was now in darkness, but Jack sounded wide-awake. Wide-awake and reflective. Something Ellery was getting used to. When presented with his own mysteries, Jack was like a dog with a bone. The difference was, in Jack's line of work, crime was plentiful but rarely mysterious.

Ellery murmured, "It must have been lodged somewhere."

"Maybe."

"As the ship disintegrates, slowly but surely, it's been working its way loose."

He felt rather than saw Jack's nod.

"Jack."

"Hm?"

"You can't blame yourself for something completely out of your control."

"No, I know." Jack's mouth brushed Ellery's temple. "Thank you."

"Yeah, but it's the truth. I know you, Jack. You feel responsible for…everything."

Jack made a sound of amusement. "Well, not *everything*."

Ellery said stubbornly, "This diver probably died before you were even born. But even if he didn't, even if he died on what you consider *your watch*, it's not your job to be everywhere all the time. There's a reason Pirate's Cove has a police department and not a-a one-man band."

This time Jack laughed out loud—earning another of those human-sounding moans from the foot of the bed. Jack scooped an arm under Ellery's shoulders, pulling him close. He said softly, "You're good for me, you know that?"

"I think so."

"Am I good for you, do you think?"

Ellery said doubtfully, "I *think* so."

Jack grinned, bent his head, said against Ellery's lips, "You really *are* a terrible actor."

A sure sign you were getting comfortable with someone was when you went back to wearing your dental retainers in bed.

Ellery popped the plastic molds out, rinsed them, dropped them into their case, and began brushing his teeth. Quietly. If he tiptoed around the bathroom, he could usually make it all the way through his shower before Watson woke up and began demanding breakfast. Once Watson was awake, everyone in hearing distance was awake, so Ellery made haste.

Over the past few weeks, he and Jack had fallen into a comfortable pattern of domesticity. Not that Jack spent every night at Captain's Seat, but he spent enough that the old house felt a little empty on those nights he slept in the village.

The mornings Jack slept over, Ellery did his best to get into the shower and downstairs first. Jack liked to show his appreciation by fixing Ellery breakfast, and his cooking skills were pretty much nonexistent. In fact, following his recent attempt to make "California omelets," it was a wonder the United Egg Association—or even the State of California—hadn't filed an injunction against him.

Okay, a little bit of an exaggeration, but the practice of preparing food for human consumption was not in Jack's skill set. Which was kind of a relief. Until Ellery had tried Jack's cooking, he had been very much afraid Jack was great at *everything*.

That Monday morning, Ellery cracked open the bathroom door to find Watson watching him from the bed with bright anticipation. Ellery put his finger to his lips. Watson climbed over Jack's legs and jumped to the floor like a skydiver hopping out of a plane.

Jack winced at the *thud* of Watson's landing, but continued to sleep peacefully on.

Ellery tiptoed out of the room, Watson trotting down the stairs after him, playfully pawing at Ellery's heels in a possible attempt to collect on life insurance. Once they reached the kitchen, Ellery let the pup out the back door, put the coffee on, fixed Watson's breakfast, and then set about fixing a summer-veggie frittata for Jack and himself.

One of the nice things about island life was that a lot of their food was home grown. Ellery had eggs straight from the chicken, as well as farm-fresh leeks, squash, and herbs for the skillet.

A bird outside the window trilled a cheery little song as Ellery sautéed the leek for three minutes, added asparagus and cooked that for another minute, then sprinkled in frozen peas and baby spinach.

He opened the back door for Watson, who returned from patrol, looking muddy and self-satisfied.

"Hm." Ellery narrowly eyed those damp paws. "You better not have been digging up my new roses."

Watson made no reply, heading straight for his dish. He began wolfing down his breakfast.

Ellery whisked together the eggs and yogurt, seasoned to taste, and poured the mixture into the skillet. He watched it bubble and cook for a few more minutes, then crumbled some goat cheese on top and popped the whole thing in the oven.

"So what are you up to today, buddy?" he asked. "Got any plans?"

Watson wagged his tail, continuing to gulp down his food as though this might be his last ever meal. Which was the way he approached every feeding. Probably the result of being abandoned.

Overhead, Ellery could hear Jack moving around, could track Jack's every action through the squeak and groan of the house's antiquated plumbing. That was something he'd address if he had unlimited funds: the plumbing. He was not looking forward to coaxing another winter out of the failing water heater.

Outside the kitchen window, the long meadow was slowly but surely turning from green to gold in the August sun. Like it or not, his first summer on the island was coming to an end.

The coffee machine beeped, interrupting his thoughts.

"It's playing my song." Jack appeared in the kitchen doorway, smelling of Ellery's bath gel and wearing the jeans and polo shirt of the night before.

"Coffee's ready and breakfast is in…" Ellery glanced at the oven timer. "One minute and thirty-three seconds." He smiled as Jack came to him, kissed him, the press of smile on smile one of the best ways to start the day. "Morning, Chief."

"Good morning." Jack was already headed for the coffee machine. "And good morning to you too," he added to Watson, who took a momentary break from sliding his empty bowl around the kitchen to look up and wag his tail.

"Hey, I've been thinking about what you were saying last night." Ellery leaned against the counter, watching Jack pour coffee into two mugs.

Jack threw him a quick look.

"Er, not that," Ellery said hastily. "Although, yes, that. For sure."

Jack bit back a smile. Then his brows rose, and he held up Ellery's *I woke up like this* Disney Princess mug.

"Film crew gag gift," Ellery said. "But it's a good-sized mug."

Jack smirked. "That's what they all say."

"*We* are *not* amused," Ellery said in his best—meaning worst—Princess of the Realm voice.

"Sure you are."

"Anyway, the obvious question is, is anyone from Pirate's Cove unaccounted for?"

"You mean, has anyone from Pirate's Cove gone missing in the last sixty years or so?"

"Right. Well, besides Rebecca Witherspoon." Given that Rebecca was no longer missing.

Jack shook his head. "I can't speak to the last sixty years, but no missing persons reports have been filed since I've been police chief."

"What about tourists?"

"Including tourists."

"What about cold cases?"

Jack grimaced. "No unexplained disappearances that still come up in conversation. I plan on deep-diving through the storeroom files today, but I'm not pinning my hopes on Chief Ballard's record keeping."

Jack's predecessor had not been much for murder-book maintenance or evidence storage. Fortunately, there wasn't a lot of crime on Buck Island—barring the occasional murder—so reopening cold cases had never been a thing.

The oven timer went off. Ellery reached for a mitt, opened the oven, and pulled out the sizzling pan. The fragrant scent of roasted herbs filled the kitchen.

"How long was Ballard chief of police? If that diver dates back to the *Roussillon*, he probably predates Ballard."

"That could be true." Jack opened the fridge, took out a bottle of sweetened oat milk and the small carton of half-and-half Ellery kept on hand for him. He diluted their coffees to specification, then handed the *I woke up like this* mug to Ellery.

Ellery said, "What about the possibility that the diver was from a salvage ship operating illegally, so he was never reported missing. Or maybe the salvage ship was operating legally, but the diver wasn't reported missing on the island because the company was based on the mainland. Maybe he was reported missing on the mainland."

"If he was reported missing on the mainland, we'd certainly have heard about it."

"Okay. But again, maybe he wasn't reported missing because he was somewhere he shouldn't have been."

Jack nodded in a *maybe yes, maybe no,* and sat down at the table. Ellery dusted dried herbs over the baked egg and vegetables, and carried the pan to the table. He cut a slice of frittata with the spatula and deposited it on Jack's plate.

Jack picked up his fork. "If this tastes even half as good as it looks and smells..."

Ellery shoveled a slab of egg and veggie on his own plate, set the pan on the trivet, and sat down across from Jack.

"Of course, there's still the possibility that the diver went down with the *Roussillon.*"

Jack chewed, swallowed, and said, "How do you figure that?"

"Let's say something happened, and this guy, a member of the crew or maybe a passenger *or* maybe even a stowaway, wasn't able to get off the ship in time. Maybe he thought his only chance of escape was to use the diving suit, but even though he got to the suit, he still couldn't get off the ship."

"No tanks, no hoses," Jack reminded him.

Ellery thought it over. "Well, maybe it's like we've been discussing. Maybe the hose rotted away, maybe he got stuck and had to get rid of the tanks, but then still couldn't get out. Maybe he didn't understand how the suit worked."

Jack's expression was skeptical. "You're reaching."

"Which part?"

"All of it."

Ellery considered, nodded. "Sure, but just because my theory is far-fetched doesn't mean it isn't possible."

"Actually, it kind of does." Jack was amused.

"Anything's possible."

Jack shook his head. Said with the confidence of long and depressing experience, "No. Not really."

CHAPTER FOUR

"There's something about him I don't trust," Nora said.

Ellery and Nora were having their morning coffee on the little wooden bench inside Crow's Nest. The picture windows offered a dazzling view of the cove, blue water sparkling, white boats rocking on the rush of morning tide, their colorful pennants snapping in the breeze. At this time of the day, the village streets were still mostly empty. The harbor master made his rounds, putt-putting around the cove in his small red motor boat. The faint *buzz* of the engine and the *clang* of buoys rocked by the incoming tide were the only sounds to disturb the sleepy silence.

This wasn't the first time Nora had expressed her reservations about their newest crew member, Kingston Peabody, and Ellery studied her profile curiously.

Nora was a small, lively woman of—in her words—*advanced years*. She had steely gray eyes that missed very little, and favored sensible shoes and a businesslike ponytail that reached all the way to the middle of her back. Her general demeanor was sharp and no-nonsense. But that was a false reading, because she was extremely kindhearted, a bit sentimental, and, in Ellery's opinion, full of fanciful ideas.

Fanciful or not, she was a good judge of character, so he didn't want to brush off her concerns, although he'd yet to hear anything particularly...concerning.

He nodded, sipped his coffee, asked, "What is it about Kingston you don't trust?"

Nora didn't hesitate. "To begin with, he knows so much about the island. So much about the village."

"He did say he used to vacation here with his wife and daughters."

Nora sniffed, unappeased.

"Why do you find that suspicious?"

"Mostly, I find it irritating. When visitors ask about the island, he's always jumping in with his opinions and ideas."

"I see. So he's giving bad or misleading information to our customers?"

"No," Nora admitted. "He really does know the island like he was one of us. He's a *complete* know-it-all."

Ellery hid his smile behind his coffee cup. "Right. Well, that would be irritating."

"To the resident know-it-all?" Nora's tone was tart. "I don't deny it."

Ellery didn't bother hiding his smile that time. "Okay. Besides, er, cultural appropriation and being a complete know-it-all, what else do you suspect Kingston of?"

Nora scowled. "Everything. And nothing." She smiled reluctantly at Ellery. "Oh, I know, I *know*. You think I'm being unfair." She sighed. "I know you like him."

"I do like him. He's helpful and knowledgeable and seems to really enjoy the job."

"I agree," she said gloomily.

"And with Felix leaving for college, we need the help."

"We might not need help in the fall. Business will slow down then."

"True." Ellery was hoping it wouldn't dwindle to where it had been last February when he'd inherited the Crow's Nest. Another winter like that might not be survivable. He said instead, "Speaking of Felix, how was his last day? Did he get his Bon Voyage card?"

Nora looked ever so slightly uncomfortable. "It was busy but not too bad. I had a Historical Society meeting to attend, so Felix offered to close up for me."

"Oh?"

For the last few years, Pirate's Cove's Historical Society had existed solely online. Nora was determined to use the occasion of their 100th anniversary to drum up the support she would need to find a new home for her beloved organization.

"He did get his card. And he was very appreciative. I think it meant a lot. Not the money. The thought."

It was hard to say what the Jones family finances were like these days, what with legal fees and divorce settlements, but yes, for Felix it would be the thought that counted. Even Kingston had donated to Felix's going-away gift, which, in Ellery's opinion, was another point in his favor.

"Then Felix closed yesterday evening?"

Ellery's tone was neutral, but Nora read his thought correctly. "I felt guilty making him close on his final day, but with the anniversary celebration next weekend, I felt I *had* to be at the meeting."

"Sure," Ellery said. "But that just reinforces my belief that we need the additional help. I mean, if you'll recall, it wasn't easy finding Kingston."

They both jumped guiltily as someone rapped briskly on the front-door glass. Watson, who had been dreaming peacefully beneath the bench, scrambled over their feet, barking hysterically.

Arf! Arf! Arf!

Ellery ordered, "Watson! No. NO." Nora put her hands over her ears. Watson ignored them both, the tone, if not the volume, of his barks changing as he recognized Jack's familiar figure standing on the front stoop of the bookstore. He—that would be Watson, not Jack—began to jump up and down.

Ellery, though more restrained, was also pleasantly surprised.

The brass bell chimed cheerily as he unlocked the door and opened it.

"Hey."

"Hey." Jack was in uniform, so he'd already swung by his cottage and changed. He'd slapped on his own Jack Black aftershave and was all business. "Do you have that letter?"

The anonymous hate mail. Right. As much as Ellery would have liked to forget about it, he appreciated the fact that Jack had not.

"It's in my office. Hang on a sec."

As Ellery made for the back office, he heard Jack's stern, "Quiet, Watson." And then, "Morning, Nora."

Nora chirped, "Morning, Chief!"

Ellery retrieved the letter, preserved in a plastic baggie in his desk drawer, and brought it to Jack.

Jack took the plastic bag, grimly studied the envelope.

"Like I said, I didn't realize what it was at first, so my fingerprints are all over it."

"Got it. I'd like you to put together a list of everyone you've had any kind of run-in with since you arrived on the island. No matter how small, how trivial, I want to know."

"The only person I've had a run-in with is Sue."

Sue Lewis was the editor and owner of the *Scuttlebutt Weekly*. From the very first, she and Ellery had butted heads. But at the moment, Sue had bigger problems than Ellery.

Jack seemed in agreement, because he said briefly, "This isn't Sue's style."

"I know, but there really isn't anyone else."

Jack said, "There's Ned Shandy. There's Cyrus. There's—"

"Okay, okay. I didn't think you meant the obvious suspects."

"I mean any and all suspects you can think of. Maybe someone who applied for a job at the Crow's Nest. Maybe an unhappy customer."

"*An unhappy customer?*" Ellery was incredulous.

"Or maybe you were the unhappy customer. Maybe you returned a drink or a meal or complained about the service somewhere."

Ellery shook his head. "I mean, I'll try and come up with some possibilities, but it's hard to believe someone wants me dead because I complained they were out of oat milk."

"We're not dealing with a rational person. Or at least, we're looking for someone who might outwardly seem rational but has a screw loose."

Ellery said dryly, "Is that the legal term for it?"

"The legal term is stalking." Jack was curt.

Well, that sure took the fun out of the morning.

Jack said, "I want to know about any encounter that left you feeling uneasy or uncomfortable, however insignificant or unimportant."

"Like this one?"

Jack opened his mouth, and Ellery said hastily, "I'm kidding. This is worrying, so I'm joking."

Jack's expression softened. "I understand. But I'll get to the bottom of this. You don't have to worry."

"I know." But of course, he was worried.

"It wouldn't hurt to ask Nora if she can think of anyone who might want to harm you."

Ellery smiled faintly at the idea of Nora as a police informant, but if anyone had her ear to the cobblestones, it was Nora. He nodded.

"Last but not least. Security cameras." Jack looked stern again. "We've talked about this numerous times. If you'd had cameras installed, we'd already have a pretty good idea of who we're looking for."

"Thanks for not saying I told you so."

"I did tell you so, and I'm going to keep telling you so until you get the damned cameras installed."

"All right, already! I'll phone today."

"Thank you," Jack said tersely.

"You're welcome," Ellery shot back.

They scowled at each other. Jack's cheek suddenly creased in a reluctant grin.

"Are you really mad at me for worrying about your safety?"

Ellery let out a long breath. "No. I don't know why I'm irritated, because you're right. I should have installed cameras months ago."

"If it's the money, maybe I can—"

"No." Ellery was adamant. "You already paid for my car repairs."

"That was your birthday gift."

"In advance and way too generous. So no. I'll figure it out." Ellery offered a lopsided smile. "But thank you. For all of it. Especially for the worrying about my safety."

Jack smiled back. "You're welcome." His light gaze flicked past Ellery. He put a hand on Ellery's shoulder, drew him in for a quick kiss. "You have a good day."

"You too."

Jack grunted. Today was the start of Buck Island Race Week, and it was going to be all hands on deck for PICO PD until the following Sunday. Which meant there was a strong chance Jack would be sleeping in his own bed until further notice.

Ellery sighed as he closed the door behind Jack. He started to relock it, then realized it was time to officially open. Nora was already at the front desk, counting the register. Watson, paws on the window, gazed wistfully after Jack's departing figure.

Ellery flipped the CLOSED sign to OPEN and joined Nora at the counter. He said briskly, "So who do you think the diver is—was—that Jack and I found on the *Roussillon*?"

Nora brightened. In her opinion, there was nothing like a nice, juicy, real-life mystery to take your mind off your troubles. "That's the question, isn't it?"

"One of them, for sure."

"I've been thinking a lot about it."

"That, I never doubted."

She didn't even hear him. "And I believe this is a case for the Silver Sleuths."

Ellery stopped smiling. "I hope you're kidding."

Nora's gray eyes rounded in surprise. "Why no, dearie. I'm not kidding. Who better to suss out the identity of this poor soul? Why, between us, the Silver Sleuths have more than five hundred years' experience of this village."

"How do you figure that? Your timelines run concurrently. Besides which, maybe you've forgotten what went down at the Black House less than a month ago? I haven't. And Jack—Chief Carson—sure as heck hasn't."

"Now, now." Nora waved off Ellery's reminder as she would a pesky sand fly. "I'm not suggesting we resume field operations."

"I-I can't tell you how relieved I am," Ellery said faintly. *Field operations?*

"But I believe if we put our thinking caps on, we'll come up with a solution as to who that skeleton is—er, belongs to. *Belonged* to. In any case, my money's on Vernon Shandy."

Question: was your skeleton you? Or did your skeleton *belong* to you? Ellery sorted through the phrasal verbs and philosophical quandaries. "Shandy? Was this Vernon a relation to Ned Shandy?"

Nora's brows drew together as she considered. "I believe Ned would be Vernon's second cousin once removed. There've been Shandys on this island as long as there have been Starlings or Sweenys. Or Pages, for that matter."

"Why do you think this diver might be Vernon?"

"Vernon was a navy diver. He disappeared while on leave."

"Disappeared?"

"Yes."

"Like…disappeared in a diving accident?"

"No. I mean he disappeared and there was never any explanation as to how or why."

Ellery said slowly, "He disappeared while he was on leave here? On the island?"

Nora nodded.

"He went AWOL and there was never any explanation?"

"Correct."

"When was that?"

"Some time in the 1960s."

"The time frame's right, I guess. But what makes you think Vernon didn't just take a ferry to the mainland and then headed to Canada?"

"No. He wouldn't have done that."

"Why not? Plenty of others did."

Nora wrinkled her nose. "It's difficult to explain. You have to understand the island culture back then. Original families like the Shandys didn't leave. Or at least, it was very rare. Leaving the island would be like emigrating to another country. You might serve in the military—many of our lads did—but they *always* came home."

"Okay, but in the 1960s, a lot of people felt differently about serving in the military."

"True. But not Vernon. Vernon volunteered for active duty. He loved the navy. He loved traveling, he loved adventure, and, frankly, he loved fighting."

"Pirate stock," Ellery guessed. That was the usual explanation islanders gave for behavior the rest of the world found hard to understand.

"Exactly."

"But I still don't understand. Wouldn't people, his family, know if Vernon went diving and never came back? Wouldn't that be reported as a diving accident?"

"Well... We're talking about the Shandys."

Yeah, Ellery had an inkling or two regarding the Shandys. They were not keen on law enforcement, for one thing. Understandably. But didn't that merely add weight to his theory? Wasn't it possible that Vernon had maybe got into legal trouble and been forced to emigrate?

"I know they own the Deep Dive."

The Deep Dive was a locals-only hangout with a shady reputation. During the summer months, more locals migrated to the tourist-free Deep Dive, but when the seasonal visitors cleared out, everyone headed back to the law-abiding comforts of the Salty Dog.

"They also own the island's only marine salvage company."

"*Ah-ha!*" Ellery said. "The doubloon just dropped. They started out as wreckers."

Nora beamed. "Very good, dearie! Yes. That's exactly right. The Shandys' original family enterprise was wrecking."

That made perfect sense. Wrecking was the practice of taking valuables from a shipwreck which foundered or ran aground close to shore. Once upon a time, it had been a mainstay of far-flung coastal communities like Pirate's Cove. According to legend, some wreckers even lured ships to their doom, using decoys like fake signals and false lights. There were some terrific stories about Buck Island wreckers in Nora's cherished copy of K.K. Peabody's *Ghosts of Buck Island.*

"I'm guessing the Shandys take a proprietary interest in the coastal waters around the island."

"Very much so. Though they're not as aggressive in protecting their interests these days. Not only is marine salvage subject to more rules and regulations, Chief Carson is *much* more diligent about enforcing the law than any of his predecessors.

That also made sense. Pirate's Cove's previous police chiefs had all been island born and bred. It was highly possible a more sympathetic, if not blind, eye had been turned to many of the Shandys' less than legal activities.

Ellery said, "So you think—or you think the Shandys thought—that Vernon might have been illegally scavenging the *Roussillon*, and that's why he wasn't reported missing?"

"I think it's more than possible."

"But if no one ever reported Vernon missing, how do you know he is? Maybe he did move to Canada."

Nora said patiently, "The navy reported him missing. The navy listed him as UA and then eventually as a deserter."

"Oh. Right. And no one has seen him since that fateful but unspecified day in 1960-something?"

"Correct."

"Hm. I can't argue that Vernon sounds like a very likely candidate for our body in Buccaneer's Bay. Would he have been so foolhardy as to go diving alone?"

"Oh yes." Nora had no doubts about that.

"But when he didn't come back, wouldn't someone have gone looking for him?"

"The best divers on the island," Nora said. "The Shandys would have searched high and low for him. They would have scoured that ship. But when they didn't find him, they would have moved on to their next priority, which would be hiding whatever he'd been up to." She shrugged.

Nora was making a pretty good case for casting Vernon Shandy as the body in Buccaneer's Bay. But if the Shandys, arguably the best divers on the island, had scoured the *Roussillon,* why *hadn't* they found Vernon?

Well, maybe that could be explained. Maybe Vernon had got himself stuck somewhere inaccessible, and it had taken time and the shifting and resettling of the wreck to dislodge him?

The good news was, if it was Vernon, his death was most likely an accident, not murder. Except... The missing hoses and tanks were still a question mark. And why had Vernon chosen to dive in that very old suit? Surely a navy diver would have access to better equipment. Surely the Shandys would have access to better equipment.

Ellery was about to ask Nora about that, but the bell pealed in welcome as the front door swung open. A petite woman of perhaps forty cautiously entered the bookshop. She wore an expensive but not particularly flattering beige pantsuit. Her stiffly styled blonde hair was as shiny and untouchable as a doll's. Her eyes were also doll-like, being round and blue and rather blank.

"Good morning!" Ellery and Nora chorused.

The woman studied them, blinked her false eyelashes, and said, "Mary Daheim."

Ellery resisted the temptation to reply, *Merry Daheim to you too!*

"Joanne Fluke, Laura Bradford, Carolyn Hart, Jenna Bennett, Nancy Atherton, Sara Rosett," rattled off the woman, still unblinking, still unsmiling.

"Cozies?" Ellery looked to Nora for confirmation.

Nora threw him the sort of look a professor bestows on a slow but earnest student. "Two aisles to your left, dear. Let me know if you need help finding a particular title."

Without a word, the woman vanished into the canyon of towering shelves. Watson gave up brooding over Jack, and followed her.

Ellery and Nora exchanged looks.

"What do your parents think of Pirate's Cove?" Nora asked politely.

Ellery quoted, "*Quaint. Very quaint.*"

"Not entirely undeserved."

"No. They're right. But—" Movement out of the corner of his eye made Ellery glance toward the Cozy section. The blonde woman stood at the end of the aisle, but she was not browsing for books. She was staring at them.

"Need some help?" He started to come around the tall wooden counter, but the woman motioned him away.

"No, no. I'm just looking." She ducked back down the aisle.

What in the world?

"Right. Okay. Well, yell if you need us." He arched his brows inquiringly at Nora. Nora pursed her lips in prim disapproval.

"Speaking of my parents, I'm having lunch with them at one. When is Kingston coming in?"

As if he didn't know. But he was uncomfortably aware of their customer hiding behind the bookshelves and listening to every word they said.

"Twelve thirty." Nora also sounded like she was enunciating for the back rows.

"I remember you!"

Ellery and Nora started as the customer popped out of the Cozy aisle, pointing in apparent accusation.

Oh no, Ellery thought. It even went through his mind that here might be a possible connection with that poison-pen note he'd received. Perhaps this woman was an unbalanced fan. Or former fan. Granted, the target audience of the *Happy Halloween! You're Dead!* franchise was typically male and about a decade younger than himself. He'd been in his midtwenties when he'd played unlucky-in-love-and-everything-else teenager, Noah Street.

But the woman was not looking at him. She was looking at Nora.

"I used to come in here all the time back then. It's really changed." She glanced around the recently renovated bookshop with its newly sanded floors, gleaming windows, and sail-white walls. "It's very clean."

"When was that, dear?" Nora inquired.

"About twelve years ago."

Nora smiled kindly. "I'm afraid you're thinking of Eudora Page. She used to own the Crow's Nest. Sadly, she passed away last winter. This is Ellery. Eudora's nephew. He runs the bookshop now."

Eudora's great-great-great-nephew, but who was keeping score?

It seemed their customer was about as sentimental as she was observant, because she immediately turned to Ellery. "You're the one I wanted to speak to."

Ellery said warily, "Uh…okay."

"I'm Odette Wallace."

She was clearly expecting a response. Ellery said, "Nice to meet you."

"I want to hire you."

"For what?"

Odette looked at him as though he were an idiot. "As an amateur sleuth, of course. Someone is trying to kill me."

CHAPTER FIVE

Beside him, Nora sucked in a sharp breath.

"That's awful," Ellery said, and meant it. "But I'm not a bodyguard. I'm not any kind of professional detective. You need to talk to the police."

Nora cleared her throat.

"I *know* you're not a bodyguard," Odette said impatiently. "I know you're not a professional. You're an *amateur* sleuth, which is what I need." For emphasis, she gestured in the direction of the Cozy section.

Had she mistaken the works of Julie Hyzy and Katherine Hall Page for True Crime?

"Amateur," Ellery agreed. "Which means I don't take *cases*. I'm not for hire. If you really believe someone is trying to kill you, you *have* to talk to the police. They can protect you."

Nora cleared her throat more loudly.

"No, I can't talk to the police. That's out of the question. And yes, you *do* take cases. Kezzie Harwood told me the only reason Julian Bloodworth isn't sitting in a prison cell right now is because *you* solved the murder of that horrible Brett Ainsley."

Wellll, okay, Ellery *had* solved that murder. He ascribed his success to being baked on painkillers at the time. Not that he was going to confide that to the peculiar Mrs. Wallace.

"That was different."

"*Ahem.*" Nora tried to catch Ellery's gaze.

"I'm sure all your cases are different. Anyway, I already know who's trying to kill me."

"You—? Then why are you—why aren't you going to the police?"

Mrs. Wallace grew more impatient. "I *mean*, I've narrowed it down. It's one of my three horrible stepchildren. Probably Vanessa. She's always hated me. They all do."

And who could blame them? But, of course, Ellery didn't say that.

"Mrs. Wallace, I…appreciate your…your confidence in me, but I'm not the guy you need. Believe me. You have *got* to go to the police. If you want, I can talk to Chief Car—"

"Name your price."

Ellery closed his mouth.

In his entire life, no one—no one who could actually make good on such an offer—had ever spoken those magic words to him. Not that he had a price, but given time to consider, he was pretty sure he could come up with one. It would probably be something like the cost of a new roof for Captain's Seat.

Nora snapped out, "Five hundred dollars an hour plus expenses. He requires a five-thousand-dollar retainer up front."

Ellery swung around to stare at her, but Nora was steely in her resolve.

"Take it or leave it."

"*Huh?*" For a second Ellery thought Nora was talking to him.

"Done," Mrs. Wallace said.

Ellery turned from Nora to Mrs. Wallace—and then back to Nora. Nora, pink-cheeked and slightly flustered, nonetheless held her ground. Her gray eyes were defiant. Well, defiantly sheepish. Or sheepishly defiant.

With great restraint, Ellery said, "Mrs. Wallace, may I have a word in private with my…my associate?"

"Of course. But please make it quick. I have to be somewhere."

Didn't everybody? Wasn't that one of the rules of existence?

Ellery jerked his head toward the back office. Nora led the way, spine ramrod straight, ponytail swinging. Far from seeming chastened, insubordination squeaked from every step of her rubber soles.

Ellery closed the office door behind them and demanded, "Nora, have you completely taken leave of your senses?"

Great, now he was starting to *talk* like someone in a cozy mystery!

Anyway, he was wasting his breath. Nora's eyes glowed with jubilation. "Our—er, *your*—first official case!"

Ellery spluttered, "What? Are you— *No*. I'm not a detective! I told you after everything that happened with Mrs. Blackwell that I didn't want to be involved in any more mysteries!"

"But you *are* involved."

"I am now! Or at least I am until I can explain things to Mrs. Wallace."

"But *think*. This is the very thing."

"The very *what* thing?"

"The very thing we've been waiting for."

"*Nora*—"

She actually made shushing motions. "Now, now. It's not as though it would be dangerous."

"You don't know that. We haven't even heard her story yet. If someone's really trying to kill her, it *could* be dangerous."

"But that's all right—"

Ellery did a double take. "Uh, no. It really isn't."

"We could set parameters. We could tell her we—you—don't do any rough stuff. We simply collect all the information, analyze the facts, and offer our—your—conclusions."

Ellery groaned, "She's as good as dead."

Nora seemed stung. "Pshaw! What an attitude. We haven't failed to solve a case yet."

"Nora, we've never had a *real* case. We've just stumbled into things and managed to not get killed as we fumbled our way through."

"And it's worked like a charm!"

"No." Ellery shook his head. "Absolutely not. This is crazy."

Even as he spoke, he thought longingly of that five grand retainer. The things he could do with that money…

Maybe Nora read that regret in his face, because she said, "Do we need the money or not?"

"Of course we need the money. We always need money. But I'm not a detective. And, despite what you imagine, neither are you."

"And yet, with the help of the Silver Sleuths you've solved no fewer than *five* crimes that previously baffled our police."

Ellery winced, imagining what Jack would have to say to that. "The police weren't *baffled*, and your numbers are *way* off."

Nora raised her hand as though to begin counting down his greatest hits, and Ellery hurried on. "If Mrs. Wallace is right, her life is in danger. We're not equipped to handle that. And even if we were, I don't want that responsibility. Do you?"

That seemed to give Nora a moment's pause. But a pause was all it was, because she said, "But since she won't go to the police, we're her best line of defense. We could do some real good here. We could save a life."

"What we need to do is convince her to go to the police."

Nora shook her head. "There's no way. After what happened when Mr. Wallace died? Never. And I can't say I blame her for not trusting the police. Even though Jack Carson wasn't chief at the time, I don't know that he'd see things any differently."

"See what things differently?" Ellery asked suspiciously. "What happened after Mr. Wallace died?"

Nora's smile was the facial expression equivalent of a pat on the head. "I forget sometimes you've only lived on the island a few months. The police arrested Odette for murder. The charges were eventually dropped for insufficient evidence, but no other suspect has ever been named."

Yikes.

Ellery said weakly, "Great. Our first client is the prime suspect in the murder of her husband."

"Which is why she can't go to the police."

"I don't follow the logic. What does one thing have to do with the other? If someone is trying to kill her—"

Ellery broke off as Mrs. Wallace knocked on the office door. "Are you still in there? I have to meet my lawyer for breakfast. Can we get this settled? I'll write you a check right now."

Ellery hesitated. Visions of greenbacks danced before his eyes—followed by the vision of Jack's disapproving countenance. On the other hand, Jack really wanted him to install security cameras. This was one way to make that happen.

"You could finally afford that security system for Captain's Seat. That would be a big relief to Chief Carson," Nora suggested with eerie perception.

"Helloooo?" Mrs. Wallace sounded increasingly testy.

"I swore I wasn't going to let you drag me into another of these crazy escapades," Ellery muttered.

Nora patted his shoulder in a *there-there-dearie.* Her eyes gleamed with excitement.

Ellery swore softly, opened the office door, and found Mrs. Wallace waiting. Watson, cuddled in her arms, wagged his tail.

Mrs. Wallace said accusingly, "I was beginning to think you'd run out the back."

If. Only.

"Not at all," Ellery assured her. "We were just discussing...logistics."

Watson, pink tongue lolling, laughed silently up at Ellery.

* * * * *

"It's just...a cop," Ellery's mom murmured.

Some of Ellery's happiness faded. "You don't like Jack?"

They were having lunch in the Seacrest Inn's cute greenhouse-style café. The dining room, with its white and black diamond floor, red leather booths, and calendar-perfect view of the cloudy sky and white-capped harbor, was packed to capacity despite the fact that Race Week's opening ceremonies were taking place on the other side of the cove.

"Darling." Talia's dark eyes were troubled. That wasn't acting. She really was concerned. "I didn't say that. I don't know him. On the surface, he seems nice enough."

"*Nice enough?*" Ellery echoed.

Talia made a face—her trademark expression: a little bit contrite, a little bit mocking. "What do you want me to say? He's handsome, polite, thoughtful, and has a steady job. Oh, and he seems to adore you."

Ellery spluttered at the idea of Jack *adoring* anything. "But?"

"But nothing. As a matter of fact, I *do* like him. A lot." Talia's smile was wry. "But it's a dangerous line of work."

"Chief of Police."

"I'm sure the pay is better than the rank and file. Better than acting, for sure. But still. A police officer. That's still a potentially dangerous job. He doesn't look like he'd be happy sitting at a desk all the time."

"No. True."

"And."

"And?"

"If you get too involved with him, you're never going to move back to New York."

Ellery's smile was equally wry. "But you already know I'm not coming back to New York. I like it here. I *love* it here."

"Well, that's good news," Nan Sweeny announced, arriving with their lunches. "We can't lose our only real bookstore." She dispensed plates with speed and efficiency. "Crab salad. Wonderful choice, Mrs. Alexander. And fish and chips for you, Ellery."

Ellery asked, "How is it that Pirate's Cove's mayor is here waiting tables in the middle of Race Week's opening ceremonies?"

"Frankie called in sick."

Frankie waitressed at both the Seacrest Inn and the Salty Dog. Because so much of the island's employment was seasonal, most people needed at least two jobs to stay financially afloat.

"Oh no. That's going to be tough on Tom if she calls in sick tonight. Libby and Felix left for college this morning."

"I know." Nan spared a commiserating shake of her head for Tom Tulley. "Any word on the identity of that body you found yesterday?"

"You know, Jack was there too. I don't know why I'm getting all the credit."

Nan grinned. "All I know is, Jack has been diving out there for years, but the first time you go out, you find a body. Any theories?"

"Just lucky, I guess."

Nan gave him a chiding look. "As to the identity of that diver."

Ellery said, "I'm sure you've heard Nora's pet theory."

"You'd think. But I've barely seen Auntie this month, she's been so busy with the Historical Society's 100th anniversary celebration. I can tell you that all of Pirate's Cove believes you found Vernon Shandy."

"Do the Shandys believe it?" Ellery wasn't sure where that question came from, but Nan looked surprised, then thoughtful.

"I wonder. Even if they did, I don't suppose they'd say so." Nan smiled at Talia. "How's the salad?"

"Delicious," Talia replied. "This is a wonderful place. I know we're going to love staying here."

Nan blushed with pleasure. "I like to think so. Anything else I can get you?"

Ellery looked at his mother. "Should we go ahead and order for George?"

Talia said airily, "Oh, I meant to tell you. George isn't coming. He's spending the day with Jack."

"He's *what*?" Ellery glanced automatically at Nan, who looked equally surprised.

"George wanted to observe the day-to-day operations of a rural, small-town police department. He's never had that opportunity before."

"Why would he need that opportunity?"

Talia's brows rose. "Is there some reason George *shouldn't* spend the day with Jack?"

"Well, no. Of course not. It's just...I can't believe Jack agreed."

Nan looked impressed. "Neither can I."

Talia appeared blasé as she speared another forkful of crab salad. "Everyone loves the movie business."

"Yeah, I really don't think Jack is dazzled by the idea of Hollywood. Let alone Off-Hollywood."

"I agree." Nan winked at Ellery. "Which means he sure must think highly of *you*."

Before he could come up with a response, she'd sped off with her empty tray.

Ellery turned to Talia. "Is George seriously thinking of filming a documentary about that diver?"

"Mm." His mother was noncommittal. "That would depend on how it all turns out." She took a sip of white wine and added in apparent non sequitur, "George is very taken with the village."

Ellery was thinking that over when they were interrupted by a tall, fair-haired man who paused beside their table.

"Well, hi there, stranger!" Robert Mane smiled lazily down at Ellery. "I hear you're up to your snorkel in another mystery."

Ellery smiled back. "Hey, I've been meaning to phone you. And no snorkeling was involved."

Ellery and Robert had gone out a couple of times over the past few weeks. Robert had made it plain that he was interested in moving their friendship on to more intimate terms, but from the first, Ellery had been straightforward about his feelings for Jack. That said, he did like Robert a lot. What wasn't there to like? He was smart, entertaining, and attractive.

Robert had turned to Talia. "With those eyes and those cheekbones, you've *got* to be related. Kid sister? Secret daughter?"

Outrageously cheesy.

Talia's eyes narrowed, but then she laughed. Ellery had known she would like Robert; her sense of humor was as quirky as his. "You've discovered our secret." She offered her hand.

Ellery said, "Talia Alexander, this is my friend Dr. Robert Mane. Mom, Rob's the Medical Director and CEO of the Buck Island Med Center."

"Charmed, charmed, charmed," Talia drawled, à la Olive Neal in *Bullets Over Broadway*.

Robert got the joke, grinning as he shook hands. "The pleasure's all mine." His expression changed. "Wait a minute. Have we met?"

"It was a movie date," Ellery said. "You were wearing jeans. She was wearing angst." The toe of his mother's sandal connected with his kneecap. "*Ow.*"

Robert's green eyes widened. "*Talia Alexander. Of course.*"

"Of course." Ellery rubbed his knee.

"Why didn't you tell me your mother was Talia Alexander!"

Ellery said solemnly, "There are many things you don't know about me, Robert."

"Tell me something I *don't* know." Robert turned to Talia. "This is such an honor. *Shove* is one of my all-time favorite films."

"*Him*, I like," Talia informed Ellery.

Robert asked with quick interest, "Who *don't* you like?"

Talia just laughed and shook her head.

Ellery watched in resignation as Robert and Talia chatted films and acting for a few moments. Not that it was any surprise his mother and Robert hit it off. For one thing, Robert was all kinds of charming. For another, he was a total movie geek.

Ellery's cell phone rang. He checked the caller ID, and his heart brightened.

Jack.

Jack possibly reaching the breaking point with Ellery's kooky, quirky family.

He hastily excused himself and went through the huge French doors onto the tidy stretch of front lawn overlooking the sandy beach. Nearly every inch of shoreline seemed covered with beach towels, umbrellas, folding chairs, and tourists. And North Point wasn't even one of the island's best beaches.

Even from up here, he could hear the rise and fall of voices. Many, many voices.

He answered his cell with, "Do you need me to come and get him? Say the word."

"What?" Jack laughed. As always, that quiet sound of amusement warmed Ellery. "No. George and I understand each other."

That was a relief. If a little surprising.

Jack was still speaking. "I thought you'd want to know. We got the preliminary autopsy report. Our mystery victim did not die in a diving accident."

"He didn't?"

"No. In fact, by all indications, he didn't die in that diving suit."

"He *didn't*?"

"Negative. It looks like he was placed in the suit postmortem."

"Then how *did* he die?"

Jack's tone was dry. "If a 9mm slug rattling around in his skull is any evidence, he was shot to death."

CHAPTER SIX

"**I** hope you won't be offended if I speak frankly," said Howard King.

Ellery, seated in a teak and sling recliner chair on the sun-drenched deck of the 155-foot-long vessel known as the *Windsong* (Home Port Newport Beach, CA), replied, "I hope so too."

Mr. King was Mrs. Wallace's lawyer. He was a tall, robust man of about sixty, and innocuously handsome like someone in the background of an Ivy League rowing photo. He sported a two-hundred-dollar haircut, a superbly tailored navy blazer, and a yacht cap.

Granted, you couldn't judge a man by his yacht cap, but yeah. A yacht cap.

Mrs. Wallace sighed wearily. "Oh, Howard."

Mr. King and Mrs. Wallace were finishing off a bottle of champagne from the day's earlier festivities, which seemed to have largely consisted of members of the Buck Island Blue Water Foundation taking photos, handing each other awards, and getting sloshed.

Maybe there was something in Ellery's tone. King permitted himself a very small, very weary smile. "You must understand. This is a delicate situation."

Ellery nodded. In his experience, murder—even attempted murder—always was.

"You don't have a great deal of experience in criminal investigation, although I admit you have more than I would consider normal for someone outside law enforcement."

No argument here.

"That's his advantage," Mrs. Wallace chimed in. "That's the advantage of all amateur sleuths. They bring a fresh perspective. They think outside the box. Their goal isn't to put as many people in jail as possible."

King looked more pained than reassured. "Odette, my dear, amateur sleuths are not a *thing*, outside of mystery novels."

"Don't be horrible, Howard. Of course they *are*. You were right there when Kezzie and Locke were talking about poor Julian nearly being railroaded into prison. Amateur sleuths are everywhere, solving all kinds of crimes. And because they're not full of bias and prejudice or trapped by all the stupid rules and regulations, they're able to solve crimes the police can't." She added darkly, "Or won't."

"Actually," Ellery interjected, "we kind of are. Subject to rules and regulations. At least, I'm sure not planning on breaking any laws."

King looked relieved. Mrs. Wallace, not so much.

She said curtly, "You know, my life is depending on *you*."

Ellery *really* wished she wouldn't put it like that. He wanted to believe she was exaggerating the potential danger, but he wasn't sure. He found Mrs. Wallace a bit of a conundrum. She did not strike him as To the Manor Born, but she wasn't a bimbo. She was sort of attractive—at least, all her features were her own—but her wide face had a flattened look, as though someone had run over her with a steamroller. Maybe it came from years spent holding her tongue— and nose—and closing her eyes. She seemed reasonably intelligent, but her childlike faith in cozy mysteries and amateur sleuths was disconcerting. Not least because she did not seem like the sort of person to enjoy the quaint and gentle charms of a cozy. She seemed like the kind of person who thought she could solve all her problems by writing a check.

But in fairness to her, an awful lot of problems *could* be solved by writing a check.

King began to explain Ellery's legal obligations. Mostly they seemed to consist of keeping his mouth shut at all costs and reporting anything he discovered directly to the lawyer. King's tone implied there would be little to find and less to report. He clearly thought this was all a waste of time and money, but Mrs. Wallace was an important client.

Possibly more.

Acting had taught Ellery hyperawareness of everything from a person's microexpressions to tone of voice, cadence, and inflection. He paid attention to small gestures and to everything that wasn't said. There was just something in King's manner that wasn't deference so much as indulgence.

And something in hers that was *almost* accommodating.

He suspected she didn't tend to put herself out for others, so that could be relevant. He wished he liked her more. Not that it mattered. He was going to help her if he could. She liked dogs, so that was a point in her favor. Or rather, she liked fluffy white furballs. She had a quartet of them, growling every time Ellery shifted position or crossed his legs. At least they'd stopped barking every time he opened his mouth.

When King had finished explaining the rules and regs, he produced an NDA, which Ellery read and signed. King folded the document, stuck it in an envelope, and sat back in his chair.

Mrs. Wallace gazed at Ellery expectantly. "Now what?"

Good question. Great *question.*

"Now you explain to me why you think someone is trying to kill you."

"They've already tried three times in the last month." Mrs. Wallace drained her champagne glass and set the tall crystal flute on the bolted down table with a little *bang.*

Three times in one month? Someone really wanted her dead. And soon.

"What happened?"

She glared at the memory. "The first try was when they weakened the railing of my bedroom balcony."

"Weakened?"

"Sawed through."

Yikes. "When was that?"

She shook her head.

"You don't remember the date?" Granted, there had been several attempts on her life, but still.

King said, "It's hard to know if that was actually the first attempt because we don't know when the railing was tampered with. Odette was in Carmel for two weeks, then home for another week before she ever went out onto the balcony. So the railing could have been damaged as much as a month earlier. We can't know."

"Who had access to the balcony?"

"Everyone," Mrs. Wallace said promptly.

"Everyone in the family? You all live together?"

She shuddered. "God no. But they grew up in that house. They all have—had—keys. Any one of them could have sawed through the railing."

"Is there a security system? A gate to the property? Is there a record of any of your stepchildren visiting the house?"

"They could sneak in. The servants would all lie for them."

King winced. "My dear…"

"It's true, Howard. You know it is. It's why I'm going to get rid of all of them as soon as I can." Mrs. Wallace caught Ellery's expression and gave a harsh, flat laugh. "The servants. *And* Tristan's horrible children. Frankly, at this point I wouldn't care if they were *all* wiped off the face of—"

King cleared his throat. Loudly.

"I can't help it if I'm not a hypocrite."

Moving right along…

Ellery said, "Okay. Tell me about the second attempt on your life."

"I found antifreeze in the white-wine decanter. I'm the only person in the house who drinks white wine."

"You're sure it was antifreeze?"

"We're sure." King's expression was bleak. "I had it analyzed."

"As if that was necessary!" Mrs. Wallace made a disgusted face. "The wine had a faint green glow. I could hardly miss it."

"You could have missed it at night."

Mrs. Wallace threw King an irritated look. "I'm not drinking myself into a stupor every evening, regardless of what those little leeches think."

Defensive much?

Ellery intervened. "What date did you discover the antifreeze in the wine decanter?"

Mrs. Wallace looked skyward for her missing patience. "All this emphasis on dates. I feel like you're getting lost in the weeds."

Was she for real? Ellery glanced at Howard King. *He* was for real, no question. So, presumably, she was for real.

He said cautiously, "Am I right that it's the same problem as far as keeping track of who might have had access to the wine decanter?"

"No. That had to have happened after I got back from Carmel. But yes, any one of them could have sneaked into the house and poisoned the wine. Frankly, the servants could have done it. They have the best access."

King said mildly, "I really don't think Martha and Chester would be willing to commit murder for anyone. Or for any reason."

Mrs. Wallace shrugged. "Maybe. Maybe not. Old people can hate as good as young people." She frowned at Ellery. "Are you not going to write any of this down?"

"I have a very good memory," Ellery replied. Which was true. He had learned at an early age how to memorize huge chunks of dialogue very quickly and then accurately quote everything right back. His mother also had that particular gift, which had always made arguments in their family interesting. There's nothing like having your own words thrown back at you verbatim to further aggravate the situation.

King, perhaps realizing Ellery was starting to have doubts about Mrs. Wallace, said, "I myself witnessed the third attempt."

"Howard saved my life." Mrs. Wallace threw King a look that made the older man blush.

"I wouldn't say *that*."

"*I* would." To Ellery, she said, "They cut the brake lines of my Mercedes."

Were these attempts supposed to look like accidents? Because it would be very difficult to accidentally pour antifreeze into a wine decanter. And even the most rudimentary investigation would surely uncover a sawed-through railing or cut brake lines.

Then again, murderers tended to be optimists. You had to be optimistic, especially in this day and age of forensic investigation, to think getting away with murder was easy. Besides, killing someone—even if you were legally found not guilty—typically created as many problems for the accused as it solved.

"Does anyone else drive your Mercedes?"

"No. Well, I let Howard drive when he's with me. Otherwise, no."

King said, "We were about to drive to Mastro's Ocean Club for dinner, and I noticed a pool of brake fluid on the garage floor. Sure enough, when my mechanic checked the car over, we learned the brake lines had been cut."

"It has to be that horrible Colby. Vanessa wouldn't know a brake line from her iPhone cord, and Mason would never lower himself to crawl under a car. Even if it meant getting me out of the way."

"He could have hired someone," Ellery pointed out. That was just for the sake of argument. He had no clue—literally—as to who any of these people were, let alone their possible motives in getting rid of their horrible, er, their stepmother.

"That would be taking quite a chance," King said.

"Taking chances goes with the territory," Ellery said. "Murder is a risky business."

"I suppose so."

Mrs. Wallace said, "All business is risky these days."

To which neither Ellery nor King had a response.

The steward arrived with another bottle of champagne. He uncorked the bottle, neatly topped up Mrs. Wallace's and King's glasses, and departed. Though Ellery did not want champagne, he would have appreciated a glass of water. The afternoon was hot, and the sun glittered on the water and bounced off every shining bit of steel and white metal.

Mrs. Wallace sipped her champagne and made a face. "I prefer it when they shake the bottle. I like the foam. I love it when the foam goes everywhere."

Ellery glanced at King, who was smiling fondly at Mrs. Wallace.

"Did you want to tell me why you believe your stepchildren are trying to kill you?" Ellery asked.

"Money." That was King.

Mrs. Wallace said bitterly, "They've always hated me. The money is just a bonus."

King said, "Odette was Tristan's second wife. Vanessa was already married by the time they met. Colby was finishing college. Mason was starting college. They weren't little children. Their mother, Kimberly, the first Mrs. Wallace, died after a long illness. There was no question of infidelity or any reason for resentment."

"And yet," Mrs. Wallace said.

King gave another of those pained smiles. "It's true that relations have not been cordial; however, I'm not convinced they're so *un*cordial that any of the children would actually attempt to harm Odette."

"You're not?"

Mrs. Wallace glared into her champagne glass.

King said, "Someone *is* trying to kill her. There's no question of that. There's a great deal of money involved, and money is a great motivator."

Mrs. Wallace said, "Howard's known them since they were children, so of course he can't imagine them committing murder."

King looked apologetic. "I would need more proof than we have now. All we have now is motive."

"There aren't any other suspects!"

King winced. "We can't know that yet."

"Yes, we can!"

Motive was subjective. That was something Ellery had learned from Jack. What could drive one person to murder might be a nonissue for another. At the same time, the most popular reasons people did away with each other could be broken down into the infamous *L* words: Love, Lust, Loathing, and Loot. Sometimes a combination.

Per Jack, who had been a homicide detective with LAPD before moving to Buck Island and taking the job of police chief, Loot, a.k.a. Greed, was by far the most frequent reason people did away with each other. And from what Ellery could observe, Mrs. Wallace had a lot of loot on her carefully manicured hands.

He interjected, "Can you give me a little background on the rest of the family?"

Mrs. Wallace looked startled and offended. "That's *your* job!"

Maybe she didn't *read* cozy mysteries? Maybe she just liked looking at those cute cartoony covers?

"Okay, but it'd be helpful to have your thoughts on each of our...our suspects. For example, you thought Colby was the most likely to have cut your brake lines. That kind of insight is useful."

Kind of an exaggeration. Honestly, Ellery wasn't sure anything that came out of Mrs. Wallace's mouth was particularly useful. In fact, he was beginning to think Nora had seriously undercharged for their services.

"Vanessa is a total snob," Mrs. Wallace said. "She thinks she's better than me because she went to fancy schools and was born in designer clothes. Of all of them, *she* hates me the most."

"Vanessa is probably the most resentful of the Wallace children," King agreed. "But she's also the least likely to act on her feelings."

"True. She prefers bitching and whining to ever getting anything done. She's big on sour faces and sulking."

King's gaze seemed to plead for Ellery's understanding.

"Right. She's the oldest?" Ellery asked.

"Vanessa just turned forty," King said. "Also, she lives in Vale. Colorado. Which, in my admittedly nonexpert opinion, means her movements are more restricted than Colby's or Mason's."

"Makes sense to me," Ellery said, which earned him another look of exasperation from his client.

"Really? Because she's here *now*."

Ellery managed not to look over his shoulder. "You mean she's attending Race Week?"

"She's competing," King admitted.

"*Ralph* is competing. Vanessa is just along for the ride."

Ellery's head was starting to spin. "Who's Ralph?"

Mrs. Wallace said, "Ralph is Vanessa's husband. He's no prize, but he certainly didn't deserve Vanessa. I'm not sure why you're focusing on Ralph. The smart money's on Colby."

"Okay, but—" Ellery made the mistake of shifting in his chair. The four fluffy dogs began to snarl like a little pack of Muppet-wolves.

Mrs. Wallace petted the dogs absently, ignoring all the slurs and slavering from her living lap robe. "Colby's the real threat."

Colby. That was the guy from the Salty Dog. The handsome blond man who had greeted Jack like an old friend. Dylan had referred to him as *Rowdy.* Which did not seem like a nickname bestowed on a solid citizen. Unless someone was being ironic.

Mrs. Wallace was still talking. "He's the most competent. And by competent, I mean ruthless. He's also the most shiftless."

"*Shiftless?*" Ellery couldn't think of the last time he'd heard that word outside of a Made-for-TV set in the Deep South. Besides, could you be both shiftless and ruthless? Didn't ruthlessness require a certain amount of focus and energy?

He asked with genuine curiosity, "What does Colby do for a living? Do any of these people work?"

"Colby and Mason are both VPs with Wallace Industries," King said. "Vanessa remains a shareholder, but no longer works for the company. She owns a string of very successful boutiques."

"They're not *that* successful," Mrs. Wallace said. "You couldn't pay *me* to shop there."

"I don't pretend to know much about women's fashion," King admitted.

"I do, and I wouldn't be seen *dead* in anything from one of Vanessa's trashy little—"

"*Ohhh-kay.*" Ellery slapped his hands on his thighs and rose. He had to raise his voice to be heard over the instantly enraged dogs. "That's probably plenty to start with."

King also stood, calling over the dogs. "I'll see you to the tender."

Mrs. Wallace made vague shushing sounds at the dogs and said, "Really, Mason is probably who you should look at. Everyone forgets about Mason because he's such a little schnook. But he's the least likely suspect, and that's usually the way it works."

No, it really wasn't. You didn't have to have a police chief boyfriend to know that much. In real life, the most obvious suspect was, nine times out of ten, the culprit. Because HELLO.

Ellery opened his mouth, thought better of it, said only, "Right. Of course. I'll be in touch."

"I would hope so! We need to know what's going on. I'm expecting a report at least twice a day."

Twice. A. Day.

Maybe he should hurl himself overboard now and get it over with, because sitting through *this* twice a day? He wasn't going to be able to take it.

As though reading Ellery's mind, King patted his back and said briskly, "This way." As soon as they were out of earshot, he added, "Don't worry. A daily phone call will be more than sufficient for the time it takes for her to lose interest in this idea. I plan to see that she hires an actual bodyguard."

"That would be a *huge* relief."

King gave a funny laugh. "You must be desperate for money, Mr. Page. Otherwise, I can't, for the life of me, understand why you agreed to take this on."

"I own a bookstore. Of course I'm desperate for money."

"Well, it'll be worth every penny if it gives Odette peace of mind. But I'll be relying on professional security to keep her safe until this is all over."

Ellery studied King's handsome, ruddy features. "Forgive me for asking, but is there a possibility she's manufacturing these close calls?"

King looked startled and then guffawed. "*Odette?* No. No chance in hell."

"It's just that the attempts on Mrs. Wallace are all so... Well, the kind of things that happen in books."

Cozy mysteries, to be precise. In real life, people tended to shoot each other. A lot. Sometimes they stabbed each other. Occasionally, they poisoned each other or knocked each other over the head with blunt instruments. Mostly they shot each other.

Even the body in Buccaneer's Bay had been shot.

King said, "But these things must happen in real life, don't they? Isn't that where the ideas for the books come from?"

"I suppose so. Not often." Truthfully, Ellery did not read cozy mysteries. He sold bushels of them, though, so there was that.

"But murder itself doesn't happen that often."

Well... Ellery was starting to think it happened more often than he'd once thought.

"True, I guess. How likely is it that Vanessa, Colby, and Mason could gain access to Odette's home without anyone knowing?"

"Not very."

"Which is another thing that bothers me."

"Please don't underestimate the seriousness of the situation." King's tone was sober. "Someone is trying to do Odette harm, and as hard as I find it to believe one of those three would commit murder, I can't come up with anyone else who has any reason to want her out of the way." He added, "But if any of those three *were* to plan a murder, it would probably be something ridiculously cliché."

"Mrs. Wallace was considered a suspect in the death of her husband. Do the Wallace children share that suspicion?"

King was silent for a moment. He said finally, "I should be glad that you've done your homework, but this is painful territory."

Done his homework? More like skimmed the CliffsNotes.

"Money is a powerful motive. But so is revenge."

"I don't doubt it. But Vanessa, Colby, and Mason know perfectly well Odette didn't kill their father.

That wouldn't—and didn't—stop them from accusing her. But believe me when I say that if one of them is planning to kill Odette, it's not for revenge. Or at least, not revenge for Tristan's death."

If not for that, then *what*?

But King was still speaking. "I respected Tristan. I admired his business acumen. But he wasn't what anyone would term *a nice man*. And he did not raise nice children. He raised cutthroat competitors. Even if Vanessa, Colby, and Mason had been fond of Odette, they'd have probably steered the police in her direction. As it was, they were *not* fond of her. They despised her and deeply resented her influence over Tristan. *Hate*'s a strong word, but yes, Odette's probably right. They probably do hate her. Even so, the attempt to throw suspicion on her wasn't personal. From their perspective, it was simply business."

"I'm not sure I follow," Ellery said. Which sounded better than, *You lost me at multiple reasons for revenge.*

"Theoretically, as Tristan's wife, Odette had the strongest motive for wanting him dead. You see, a verdict of suicide would have made null and void a particularly lucrative clause in Tristan's insurance policy."

Ellery stopped walking. "You're saying Mr. Wallace's death was suicide?"

King also stopped. "I have no such proof."

Leave it to a lawyer. "But that's what you believe?"

"Regardless of what I believe, this entire conversation falls under the confidentiality clause you signed a little while ago."

"Understood, but are you saying *you* believe Wallace killed himself?"

King sighed. "I have zero doubt Tristan killed himself. He grew up on boats. He was far too skilled a sailor to have fallen overboard. No. He killed himself. And they all know it. But money is a very powerful incentive. Even Odette preferred being accused of murder to suggesting Tristan committed suicide."

"Yikes. But why would he commit suicide?"

King said simply, "He was dying."

CHAPTER SEVEN

By the time Ellery arrived back at the Crow's Nest, it was after four.

The bell chimed in welcome as he opened the door—and then he went staggering back as Nora barreled through.

"Goodness! Dearie, you startled me, lurking out there!" Nora exclaimed as Ellery steadied her.

"Lurking? I was opening the door."

Nora ignored that. "This is unfortunate timing. I was hoping you'd be back earlier and we could discuss the case, but there's an emergency meeting of the Historical Society. I've got to run."

Literally, it seemed.

"Okay, I guess I'll talk to you..."

He was speaking to thin air. Nora had sped away down the street as fast as her sensible shoes could carry her.

"Tomorrow," Ellery finished, and went inside the bookshop.

That was a little disappointing. He too had been hoping they could talk over some of what he'd learned during his meeting with Mrs. Wallace and Mr. King. It seemed that would have to wait.

Compared to the buzzing activity of the crowded street, it was very quiet inside the bookshop. Watson, at least, was delighted to see him. The pup jumped up and down and ran circles around Ellery, to the amusement of the handful of customers still browsing the tall shelves.

Ellery squatted down to say hello properly, managing not to overbalance as Watson pounced on him.

"Okay, okay. I missed you too." He kissed Watson's cold nose, rose, and made his way to the sales counter, where Kingston had been checking titles off a shipping invoice.

Kingston greeted him with a cheery, "Hello there!"

He was about Nora's age. A slight, spry man with longish silver hair and observant green eyes behind stylish gold spectacles. He favored bow ties and high-waisted trousers. His manners were those of a bygone era. Possibly the era of Henry James. And he knew a great deal about noir fiction and films, as well as the history of Buck Island.

"How's it going?" Ellery asked.

Kingston looked apologetic. "We've had a few regulars stop by, but most people are down at the harbor enjoying opening ceremonies."

"I figured." Ellery had a feeling it was going to be like this all week. Most of the island's current visitors were there for Race Week and only Race Week.

On cue, a customer wandered up to the counter and asked where the restroom was located. Kingston answered pleasantly. He was always pleasant, always patient.

They watched in silence as a couple of golf carts—horns honking loudly—whizzed past the large front windows. Drivers and passengers shrieked with laughter.

Kingston sighed. Ellery silently concurred.

It occurred to him he should phone Jack as soon as possible and confess—er, update him on the decision to… How *was* he going to describe this little endeavor?

It turned out to be moot, because after he excused himself and ducked into his office to phone PICO PD, he was informed that Chief Carson had stepped out but would be back in an hour or so.

Next, he tried phoning Mr. Honeycutt, the lawyer handling Brandon Abbott's estate. Mr. Honeycutt, a silky-voiced administrative assistant informed him, had left for the day but would return Ellery's call upon the morrow.

Okay, they didn't actually say *upon the morrow*, but it was an *upon the morrow* tone, and Ellery had to be satisfied with it.

He returned to the front desk, where Kingston had finished with the shipping invoice. Kingston smiled, and Ellery said, "I've been meaning to ask. How are you settling in?"

Kingston's answer was rueful. "It's different. Living here versus visiting, that is."

Yes, happy vacations spent with a wife and daughters would be very different from trying to find your place in a clannish, close-knit community like Pirate's Cove. Ellery knew that from experience. And he at least had the advantage of being descended from one of the island's oldest families.

"Are you still looking at houses?"

"Yes. There's really not much available now, but perhaps off-season."

Ellery nodded noncommittally. Real estate was always at a premium on the island.

The last of their "customers" wandered out without buying anything.

The bell on the door chimed in welcome as another person entered the bookshop—and asked to use the restroom.

Kingston directed them to the back, then caught Ellery's gaze and smiled. "Don't worry. It'll be back to normal next week."

"I hope so. It's not like there's a lot of summer left."

Or summer business.

Kingston made no response to that. He busied himself sorting through a box of used books. That was a task Nora took particular pleasure in, but Nora was not there, and Ellery couldn't see why Kingston shouldn't have the fun of panning for gold amid the dog-eared paperbacks and yellowed hardcovers.

But maybe Kingston read his thoughts, because he said after a moment, "I'm afraid Nora doesn't like me much."

It was tempting to come up with some comfortable excuse. Ellery hated confrontation. Even other people's confrontations. But he liked Kingston too much to lie.

"I'm not sure what's going on," he admitted. "Maybe she's feeling a little territorial. Or maybe it's a personality conflict. Or maybe it's something else."

Kingston looked up from the lurid covers of a trove of Mike Hammer novels, and studied Ellery quizzically for a moment.

Yeah, but that was about as close as Ellery could come to saying it. If Nora had actually spelled out *why* she didn't trust Kingston, Ellery might have tried to articulate her concerns, but he could hardly put it out there that, by her own admission without any reason or proof, Nora believed Kingston to be a shady character.

She doesn't like the cut of your jib.

That's what it would amount to.

Kingston's smile grew regretful. "Under the circumstances, I suppose there's no point in asking to join the Tuesday evening book club."

Kingston was lonely. That didn't take any deduction at all. Kingston had moved to Buck Island to start a new life, but however much he wanted to fit in, to become part of the community, it wasn't going to happen. Or at least, not any part of the community where Nora held influence.

"Maybe give it a little time," Ellery suggested.

"I'm nothing if not optimistic," Kingston assured him. He seemed a little wistful to Ellery, but then he chuckled as Watson came around one of the bookshelves, loudly squeaking his favorite green frog toy. Watson threw the frog in the air and looked expectantly from Ellery to Kingston.

Kingston said, "I think that little fellow's longing for a walk. I can man the fort if you'd like to take him."

Ellery hesitated. Other than the customer using the restroom, the bookshop was empty. Kingston could certainly handle things for a few minutes. Ellery's only hesitation was Nora's oblique suspicions, and how fair was that?

"Thanks, I'll make it short."

Kingston had returned to sorting crinkled paperbacks. He waved Ellery off absently. "Take as long as you need."

It was good to get outside. Good to be alone with his thoughts for a few minutes.

Watson pranced happily along the wharf, as though showing off his new red harness, barking a greeting to other dogs on leashes or people he recognized.

Arf! Arf! Arf!

"He's getting so big!" the woman who ran the drugstore sales counter called from across the street.

"He's eating me out of house and home," Ellery called back.

Of course, Watson was never going to be *big*, but he was growing fast, smooshed puppy face and pudgy body both lengthening, refining into… Well, he didn't seem to be any recognizable breed, but somehow all those mismatched parts melded into one adorable, if loudmouthed, dog. Ellery smiled faintly, letting the retractable leash out a little more as Watson scampered along, then hastily retracted the lead as the pup lunged in pursuit of a nearby seagull. The gull flapped its wings in bored disdain, landing safely out of reach on the white railing, and chuckling evilly as Watson barked his disapproval.

Arf! Arf! Arf!

Huoh-huoh-huoh! Huoh-huoh-huoh! retorted the gull.

"Okay, you two. Break it up." Ellery tugged at the leash, and Watson, muttering beneath his breath, finally gave up harassing the seagull.

They continued their stroll toward the pier, and Watson recovered his cheery mood, bouncing after everything from a stray windblown bee to a discarded paper cup.

What would he do if he ever actually caught anything?

Speaking of trying to catch things, despite the comfort of that fat check now sitting in his bank account, Ellery already regretted agreeing to "sleuth" for Mrs. Wallace. For one thing, he was unhappily aware of how absolutely unqualified he was to tackle a case like this. Even with Mr. King's reassurance that he would hire a bodyguard to watch over Mrs. Wallace, Ellery felt the weight of his responsibility.

"You know, my life is depending on you."

For another thing, in his previous adventures, he'd always had some kind of personal investment. His involvement had happened naturally, organically. Okay, maybe not from Jack's perspective. But from Ellery's perspective, absolutely. From his perspective, he'd been drawn into other investigations because he knew—or thought he knew—the people involved. *Or his own safety and/or freedom had been at stake.*

But he had no personal connection to this case. He didn't know Mrs. Wallace. Or Mr. King. Worse, he didn't much like Mrs. Wallace. Or Mr. King.

He certainly didn't want anything bad to happen to her, and he was (unwillingly) intrigued by the mystery she'd presented him with, but he had a lot going on right now. In addition to his parents being in town, he had to deal with the never-ending renovations at Captain's Seat; the sticky situation between Kingston and Nora at the Crow's Nest; trying to deal long-distance with Brandon's lawyer and literary agent (both of whom seemed to resent his existence); the realization that he was going to have to testify at two—TWO—upcoming bail hearings; discovering yet *another* body; and, last but probably not least, anonymous threats from a stalker.

No wonder he felt overwhelmed.

Nor had Ellery missed the fact that one of his prime suspects in the Wallace case was the guy who had greeted Jack like a long-lost friend at the Salty Dog: Colby Wallace, a.k.a. Rowdy.

Which, by the way, had to be one of the all-time most irritating nicknames.

Jack was not going to be happy if this Rowdy turned out to be Ellery's main suspect. That was a given. Then again, Jack wasn't going to be happy with any of this, so the Rowdy angle was likely irrelevant.

Honestly, if Mr. King hadn't confirmed Mrs. Wallace's story, Ellery would have been a bit skeptical about her claims of attempted murder. Not that he thought Mrs. Wallace was dishonest or overly imaginative. He hadn't seen enough of his client to form any strong opinion as to her character. No, it was more about these clumsy efforts to do away with her.

Three failed tries in less than a month was a lot. A lot of tries and a lot of failures. That alone seemed to indicate...something.

What?

Was there some time factor he was unaware of? Or had someone simply reached the breaking point?

Also, the hodgepodge modus operandi: poison, cut brake lines, sawed-through railings. *Really?* It was like the would-be murderer was just throwing things at a wall in hopes that something, anything might stick. Since there was no real effort to make these attempts look like an accident, why not be more direct?

If the would-be murderer had access to Mrs. Wallace's home, surely they had access to her person?

Either this was one squeamish villain, or they shared Mrs. Wallace's taste in crime fiction.

Or they didn't really want her dead?

Or they were really, really inept?

All of the above? None of the above?

So yeah, if Mr. King had not confirmed Mrs. Wallace's story, Ellery would have wondered if maybe his client was making all this up. But King's instant and amused reaction to that suggestion had been convincing.

Anyway, the final and most disheartening thing about taking on this case was Ellery's increasing awareness that he had no real way of solving it. He didn't know any of these people. He had no access to them. The attempts on Mrs. Wallace's life had all happened in California. How was he supposed to investigate from Buck Island? And even though it seemed that Colby, a.k.a. Rowdy, and Vanessa were both on the island now, he had no way to compel them to speak to him. Even if they agreed to an interview, he wasn't great at questioning people. He didn't like being rude, and what the heck was ruder than hinting you thought someone was trying to commit murder?

Unlike his previous forays into sleuthing, he couldn't rely on local gossip and rumor. Nora and the

Silver Sleuths weren't going to be a lot of help this time around.

His best potential resource was Jack, and he could just imagine what Jack would have to say if asked to pull some strings.

And just like that, as though conjured by Ellery's guilty conscience, Jack appeared.

Appeared, that is, in Ellery's line of sight.

Jack stood on the crowded white pier, near the walk-up window of the Gull's Wing café. In his navy-blue uniform, he was easy to spot amid the swimsuits and sun hats. He was not alone, and it didn't look like he was ordering food. He was talking to someone: a man in denim cut-offs and a red and black Aztec print short-sleeve shirt. The man's back was to Ellery, and he couldn't read Jack's eyes behind his shades, but even at that distance, he thought Jack looked somber. All Jack's attention was focused on his companion.

Watson, barely a foot high, couldn't possibly see Jack in that milling mass of people, but he knew he was there. He began tugging at his leash, and, of course, barking at the top of his lungs.

Arf! Arf! Arf!

"Watson, no," Ellery snapped. He was sure, even without being able to see the other man's face, that Jack was talking to Rowdy Wallace. True, Ellery had only glimpsed Rowdy the previous evening, but something about the set of those square shoulders and the shape of that handsome, blond head had branded itself into Ellery's memory.

Watson ignored Ellery's command, still straining at the leash, barking still more loudly.

ARF! ARF! ARF!

Even over the rush of waves hitting the pylons, the warning horn of the soon-to-depart ferry, and the din of voices, Jack recognized that bark. He glanced over his shoulder, glanced down the pier toward the avenue.

Ellery knelt, hauling Watson, who protested with a yelp, to him. "*Shush.*"

But *why*? Watson's wounded brown gaze seemed to ask. And it was a good question. *Why* had Ellery done that? Why had he ducked out of sight like he'd been caught spying? Or like Jack was doing something wrong? Too many mystery novels?

Ellery had not been spying. He had nothing to feel guilty about. And there was nothing inappropriate about standing at a food stand, having a conversation with another man. There was nothing in this situation to object to. Even if Ellery had a right to object.

Which he did not.

The last time he and Jack had discussed Their Relationship, Jack had said he did not want, was not ready, to make a commitment. Which Ellery accepted. Ellery wasn't one hundred percent sure he was ready to make a commitment either. They had only known each other a couple of months, and had only really dated for a few weeks.

Ellery had known Todd for much longer—thought he had, anyway—and things had still gone about as wrong as they could.

Maybe that was the answer right there. That unfamiliar flash of anxiety, of doubt, that had spurred Ellery to hit the ground like a kid in a drop drill, was probably way more about Todd than Jack. But understanding why he felt whatever it was he was feeling didn't make him feel it any less.

Ellery petted Watson's sleek black head, and Watson licked his chin in forgiveness.

"Sorry, buddy. Jack's busy right now. We'll visit another time." He rose, looked back at the pier, and saw Jack and Rowdy moving around the side of the Gull's Wing.

Maybe they were headed to the patio for a late lunch.

Maybe they felt they needed a little more privacy.

There was no reason to make anything of that decision to move out of sight—if it even *was* a decision to move out of sight, given that there were hundreds of people piled onto that pier—and yet Ellery's heart sank deeper than the *Roussillon*.

CHAPTER EIGHT

"**W**ell, well. I hear you found Vernon Shandy!"

In addition to being a founding member of the Monday Night Scrabblers, Stanley Starling belonged to the Silver Sleuth Book Club, so Ellery viewed that particular gleam in Mr. Starling's eyes with caution.

"I wouldn't go that far."

"But it seems you *did* go that far," cackled Mr. Starling. "All the way to the bottom of the sea. Or at least Buccaneer's Bay."

Game night was one of the highlights of Ellery's week—second only to the nights Jack slept at Captain's Seat—but he'd been tempted to skip out that evening. It had been a very long day (and not much sleep the night before), and Watson had been uncharacteristically whiny and out of sorts when Ellery had left him with his puppysitter. But as Dylan had invited Ellery's parents to join the Monday Night Scrabblers for drinks and poker, he'd felt obliged to make an appearance.

"I don't think there's been a formal identification of that skeleton," Ellery told Mr. Starling. He hadn't heard from Jack since lunchtime, but he was confident that if the lost diver had been officially IDed, Jack would have phoned.

Mr. Starling gave Ellery the raspberry for this cautious, i.e., *poor-spirited* response. "Of course it's Vernon. Who else could it be? It's no secret he spent all his free time searching for the *Blood Red Rose* and all her treasure."

"Yeah, but he couldn't have been looking for the *Blood Red Rose*'s treasure on the *Roussillon*. So what was he doing there?"

"Oh please," Janet drawled. "We all know what one of the Shandys would be doing on a sunken ship off the coast of Buck Island."

Ellery was not a poker player, so he and Mr. Starling and Janet Maples were playing Scrabble in Dylan's dining room. Ellery could tell by the groans and laughter from the poker table in the next room that his mom was cleaning out everybody's life savings. He placed six tiles on the board, spelling out SEDUCE.

Mr. Starling scowled. Janet raised her brows, murmured, "Is there something we should know?"

"Ha." Ellery always tried to dominate the left side of the board when he played his first three words. The game closed fast if you could force your opponents to migrate east, but tonight his strategy had worked against him. He drew six new tiles from the bag, and said, "The *Roussillon* sank in 1956, so there should still have been plenty to salvage a few years later."

Janet noted his score, said, "What's hard to believe is he'd go salvage diving on his own." Her four tiles made the word DOTE.

Mr. Starling said, "He wouldn't have. I remember Vernon. He was wild, sure. They're all wild in that family. And the girls are wilder than the boys! But Vernon was no fool. I've always suspected the Shandys knew exactly what happened to him."

Someone certainly knew. Whoever had put that bullet in Vernon's head—assuming it had been Vernon in that old diving suit—knew. If Jack was right about the body being placed in that suit after death, maybe there had never been any diving expedition at all. *Or* the expedition had gone very, very wrong.

So wrong that one diver decided to murder the other?

What the heck could bring about that turn of events? Especially between family members. Because that was what Mr. Starling had inferred. And he wouldn't be the only one making that deduction. Plenty of people in Pirate's Cove believed Vernon had been diving with family. But maybe he'd been diving with a buddy. He was on leave, after all. Maybe an afternoon of drinking and diving had ended in murder?

"Why would Vernon go salvaging in vintage diving dress, though?" Ellery asked.

Mr. Starling rubbed his hands together gleefully. "Yes. That's a puzzle. That's the best part of the puzzle."

Janet suggested doubtfully, "For a joke?"

The joke was on Vernon, if that was the case. "He must have had a weird sense of humor," Ellery said. "He'd be stuck with antiquated equipment the whole dive." Maybe not even complete equipment. Maybe no tanks. Maybe no hoses. No. That really would not make sense. "Where would he even find vintage diving dress?"

Mr. Starling brushed that pesky detail aside. "That's easy. The Shandys were diving these waters before anyone else. They used to have tons of that stuff lying around. They donated a bunch of it to the Historical Society back in the day."

"Back in Vernon's day?" Ellery asked.

"No, no. Come to think of it, not long before they lost their lease. Vernon was long gone by then."

Janet's brows drew together. "Who lost whose lease?"

"The Historical Society. You remember." Mr. Starling gave Janet the eyeball equivalent of an elbow in the ribs.

Janet's smile was acidic. "Oh, right. How could I forget that little wench Tommy Rider and all her shenanigans?"

"*Exactly.*"

If they thought they were speaking in code, they were mistaken. Ellery knew the whole story, via

Nora. The reason Pirate's Cove's Historical Society now existed solely online was largely thanks to some real-estate machinations that had left the organization without a roof over its head. Part of Nora's determination to make the upcoming 100th Anniversary Celebration an affair to remember was her hope that the fundraiser would provide the means to a new home for the society.

Ellery already had some ideas about that, but he was still trying to work out the details with the Abbott Estate.

"CORPSES," Mr. Starling said triumphantly, using Ellery's *S* to complete his final word.

"Yuck. I'm starting to think you're a bad influence," Janet told Ellery.

Ellery opened his mouth, but was forestalled by Dylan, who breezed into the room.

"Who needs a top-up?" Dylan called.

"We all do." Janet began to do up the final tally.

Ellery rose from the table and went to join Dylan at his well-stocked bar. Dylan briskly joggled the cocktail shaker while giving Ellery a look of reproach. "You didn't tell me your mother was a card shark."

Ellery spread his hands in a *what-can-I-say.* "You know what teachers earn? A gal's gotta make a living somehow."

Dylan chuckled. "Seriously. She's terrific. George too, although I'm not misremembering, am I? You did tell me your father was an acting coach."

"My father was an acting coach. Technically, George is my stepdad."

Dylan's expression was wry. "Your mother's right. You *are* cagey."

Ellery winced. "Not really. Careful sometimes. I didn't know you that well back then. And, you know."

"Oh, I know. People can be…tiresome."

Possibly not the smoothest of segues, but that reminded Ellery.

"So where's September tonight?"

Dylan's sigh was long and mournful. *"Mais où sont les neiges d'antan?"*

"She moved to France?"

"No. We've had a tiff." Dylan opened the cocktail shaker and poured the shimmering blue-black liquid into Ellery's martini glass.

"A *tiff*?" Ellery tried not to sound too hopeful. He didn't care much for Dylan's girlfriend. He had known a few September St. Simmons back in the day. Both male and female. Now that he thought about it, it was possible Todd had been a bit of a September Simmons. More interested in Ellery's connections than in Ellery. He said vaguely, "That's too bad."

"Isn't it?" Dylan's tone was equally vague.

Ellery couldn't in good conscience say he hoped they worked it out. He settled for, "I hope she, er, feels better. Hey, off topic, I know, but what exactly happened to Tristan Wallace?"

What he'd have liked to ask was, *What can you tell me about Rowdy Wallace?* But Dylan was too shrewd not to form his own theories as to Ellery's curiosity.

"I don't know *exactly* what happened to him. No one does. But apparently he fell off his yacht and drowned."

Ellery's interest warmed a few degrees. "Was his body ever recovered?"

Dylan's brows arched. "This is a rather grim turn of conversation. Yes, his body was recovered." A gleam of curiosity lit his blue gaze. "Why? What is it that you suspect?"

"You know me. The worst." Ellery was mostly joking. He wasn't exactly sure what prompted his curiosity. Something Mr. King had said perhaps? Something Mr. King had *not* said?

Dylan grinned. "Did you think Wallace might be the diver in the suit you found?"

"It went through my mind. But it's pretty hard to imagine how that would happen." When the Tristan Wallaces of the world disappeared, people noticed, people asked a lot of questions. When the Vernon Shandys of the world disappeared…not so much.

Ellery asked, "Was there any question that Wallace drowned?"

"I don't know, but I'd assume there were plenty of questions in a case like that. But he did definitely drown. Or at least that was the ME's verdict." Dylan's gaze was curious. "Why?"

"I just wondered. If the death was ruled an accident, why was Mrs. Wallace arrested for his murder?"

Dylan looked thoughtful. "Because it made for a more interesting story?"

"I'm not following."

"I think people were rather disappointed when Wallace's death was ruled an accident. He wasn't the type, for one thing."

Ellery said, "Anyone can have an accident."

"True, but he was an expert yachtsman."

"Even so."

"I know. But he was a very careful, precise sort of person. I think it was hard for people to imagine him falling off his yacht. *Much* easier to imagine someone pushing him." Dylan winked.

Ellery's mother strolled in from the living room. "Has the party moved in here?"

"The party is wherever you are, dear lady," Dylan said gallantly.

Ellery snorted.

"You do wonders for my ego," Talia told him.

"He's an infidel. Ignore him," Dylan said. "Another martini?"

"Are you people going to stand around gabbing all evening?" Mr. Starling shouted from the table. "Let's play Scrabble!"

* * * * *

Watson gave Ellery the cold shoulder during the moonlit drive back to Captain's Seat.

Not that fifteen minutes was such a long drive, but it felt long when your little buddy was not speaking to you.

"It's not like I planned this," Ellery protested to the silent black ball on the passenger seat. "There's just a lot going on right now."

As far as Ellery could tell, there was not so much as the twitch of a nose or the flip of an ear.

"I'm going to make it up to you. It's going to be wine, women, and long walks on the beach once my parents leave town. I promise."

Watson heaved a long sigh and buried his nose more firmly beneath his tail.

CHAPTER NINE

Moonlight gleamed in starlike points from the lightning rods atop Captain's Seat roof. The house was in complete darkness but for a single window on the lower level. Though it was unlikely the decrepit mansion had ever appeared on the cover of a gothic novel, it would have been perfect—except the solitary light should have beckoned from the tower, not the kitchen.

Not that those barefoot ladies in windswept negligees couldn't have used a midnight snack or maybe a hot buttered rum. Ellery was certainly longing for a hot drink and a bite of something more substantial than pretzels and popcorn.

He parked the VW in the front drive, got out, and went around to open the passenger door and unsnap Watson from his harness. Watson hopped down, shook himself, and trotted off across the weeds and crumbled flagstones.

Captain's Seat mansion had been built back in the 1700s by Ellery's famed pirate-hunting ancestor

Captain Horatio Page. With its blue-black granite exterior, whimsical curved gables, and jewel-bright stained-glass, the house had once been one of the grandest homes on the island. But time and the fall of the Page family fortunes had nearly reduced the place to rubble. Ellery had been working for months to simply make it livable. It would take years to restore it to its original zany glory.

He gave Watson a minute or two to investigate, then whistled to the pup and started up the steps to the front entrance.

The ship's lantern porch light shone in cheerful welcome, illuminating a wall furred with dozy winged insects. Mottled owlet moths, pink-tinged sphinxes, and giant silk moths barely stirred as he unlocked the heavy front door and pushed it open.

The scent of fresh paint and sanded wood greeted him—renovations at Captain's Seat were ongoing. The entry hall was dark. Ellery had left the kitchen light on and the warm glow from down the hall provided faint illumination, limning the O-shaped mouths of the wooden cannons carved into the balustrade overhead.

"How about a Bedtime Bone?" Ellery suggested to Watson.

Watson had other ideas, snatching up his ragged stuffed weasel, giving it a good shake, and then dropping it invitingly before the toes of Ellery's Gore-Tex boots.

Ellery sighed, picked up the weasel, and tossed it up the staircase. Watson hurtled up the stairs after the toy. They played that game for a few minutes, and then Ellery pitched the toy one final time to the top of the staircase, and headed down the long hallway to the kitchen.

He was trying to decide between cocoa and Sleepytime tea for his before-bed wind-down. As tired as he was, he felt keyed up, uneasy. He was increasingly doubtful of the wisdom of agreeing to work for Mrs. Wallace, and he wanted to talk it over with Jack, but Jack had never called him back. Which most likely meant Jack already had his hands full with Race Week revelers.

Anyway, it wasn't like they spoke every single night.

Well, actually, yes. For the past couple of weeks, they *had* checked in with each other regularly.

But during the past couple of weeks Jack hadn't been dealing with a cold—very cold—murder case or the unruly crowds of Race Week. And it was just past eleven, so Jack, who often worked late at the station, might still phone. The only reason Ellery was giving this a second thought was his suspicion—more accurately, sense—that an emotional connection existed between Jack and Rowdy Wallace. And the only reason he was giving *that* a second thought was because of everything that had happened with Todd.

He was irritated with himself for that little niggle of insecurity, but Todd's betrayal was still relatively fresh and, yeah, it *had* made him less trusting.

So that's where Ellery's thoughts were when he walked into the brightly lit kitchen and found every cupboard door wide open and every drawer pulled out and emptied on the floor.

He stopped in his tracks, trying to make sense of what he was seeing.

His first thought was, *Oh no.*

His second thought was, *Jack was right.*

His third thought was, *Great-great-great-aunt Eudora had* a lot *of pot holders.*

Even as his bewildered brain tried to process what had happened, he was backing up, groping for his phone, and...he fell over Watson, who (still squeaking the toy weasel) had come up behind him.

Watson yelped, scooting away as Ellery landed hard on the wooden floor. That...hurt. The awkward twist as he tried to avoid landing on Watson. *Ouch.* Head banging onto hardwood. *Double ouch.* He barely had time to register the pain before he rebounded, shooting upright, scrambling to his knees, and grabbing for the puppy.

"Watson. Come here, buddy."

Watson ignored him. Huff raised, he stared past Ellery at the half-open pantry door, and then he growled.

The growl was surprisingly deep, surprisingly ferocious for such a little dog, and Ellery, following Watson's fixed gaze, felt his scalp crawl in horrified recognition.

Something about the absolute motionless silence emanating from the crack between door and frame felt alive and listening.

He's still here. He's still in the house.

Ellery knew, knew without a doubt, that the intruder was hiding behind the pantry door, watching them.

Knew without a doubt that the intruder must now realize Ellery knew he was there.

Knew—

"Watson." Ellery grabbed for Watson, who began to bark in a loud, grown-up dog's voice.

RUFF! RUFF! RUFF!

This is not a drill! That was Watson's take as he ducked away from Ellery, bouncing stiff-legged, like a mechanical toy, toward the pantry.

"Watson..."

The pantry door flew open, and a large, indistinct figure, wearing a gray plaid shacket and an old-fashioned Bozo the Clown mask, burst out of the pantry and charged straight at them.

Watson lunged for Bozo, and Ellery dived for Watson, gasping, "No, boy!"

He rolled out of harm's way with the snarling puppy in his arms, watching in disbelief as the heels of the intruder's brown rubber boots flicked past his nose.

The pound of the intruder's footsteps faded as Watson wriggled and squirmed, barking frantically. "No. No way." Ellery hung on to Watson with one arm, grabbing for his phone—which Watson, in his struggles, promptly knocked out of his hand.

Ellery swore, snatched up his phone again, and thumbed in the PICO PD's afterhours emergency number. His heart was thudding, his hands shaking, as he listened to the ring on the other end. During the winter months, his call would have been rerouted, but proof of the challenges posed by Race Week, a weary female voice answered and asked what his emergency was.

Ellery gulped out his emergency, was reassured that help was on the way, and, ignoring requests to stay on the line, disconnected in order to phone Jack.

Jack answered at once with a crisp, "Hey, I'm on my way. Are you okay?"

"That was fast! I'm fine. Watson's fine. I'm not sure what's missing yet. I only got as far as the kitchen when we realized there was someone here. The kitchen looks like it was ransacked."

Jack cut across this babble of information. "You're sure you're not hurt?"

"I'm sure. He just ran out. I didn't try to stop him."

"I should hope to hell not! Okay, listen. I want you to go outside and stay there till we arrive. He might not have been working alone."

Yikes. "Right. Okay." Ellery stumbled toward the hallway, still awkwardly lugging an increasingly irate Watson.

"Did you recognize him? Did you see his face?"

"No. He wore a mask."

"Okay. I'll be there in ten."

"We'll be waiting."

The front door stood wide open. Ellery carried the frantically struggling Watson outside, down the steps, and at last half dropped, half lowered him to the ground. Watson bounded away across the gravel and straggling grass, barking his outrage.

ARF! ARF! ARF!

Ellery scanned the empty drive, searched the long expanse of meadow, but there was no sign of their intruder.

Where had he disappeared to so fast?

Nothing moved in the moonlight. Ellery tried to hear over the thump of his heart in his ears. No sound of footsteps. No sound of an engine.

Crickets. The night wind through the dead grass. Watson.

Was it possible the intruder was still there? Hiding in the shadows?

Unease slithered down Ellery's spine.

Watson's barks echoed off the granite walls and stone terraces as he vented his multiple frustrations, racing around the yard, nose to the ground, trying without success to track their midnight visitor.

That was the good news, right? Because if the intruder was still here, Watson would have probably located him by now.

Right?

Please let that be right...

The minutes ticked slowly by as Ellery waited in the dark, staring up at the forbidding facade of Captain's Seat, but eventually he caught the far-off pulse of light through the trees, the keen of sirens. The keening grew to a shriek as two white police vehicles came tearing up the drive, red and blue lights flashing, followed by the familiar outline of Jack's SUV.

The three vehicles skidded to a halt, kicking up dirt and gravel, and Jack and his officers held a quick parley out of Ellery's earshot. Officers Martin and Battye peeled away, heading into the house.

Jack strode across the wet-glistening grass to join Ellery.

"Hey."

Ellery said shakily, "H-hey yourself."

They hugged, and the unexpected tightness of Jack's arms surprised Ellery. Then Jack leaned back, his gaze dark and searching. "How're you doing?"

"All things considered, great."

Jack said grimly, "Yeah. No kidding. That could have—" He stopped, said instead, "Walk me through exactly what happened." He bent to pet Watson, who was leaping up and down to get his attention, but his gaze remained on Ellery.

Ellery hadn't got far into his recounting his adventures when Battye and Martin reappeared. Martin gave Jack a thumbs-up, signifying their confidence that no other intruders were lurking in the nooks and crannies of Captain's Seat. Which was probably correct, though the officers could have no clue how many nooks and crannies there actually *were* between those four walls. Ellery had a suspicion the house had all kinds of secrets he'd yet to discover.

Battye and Martin disappeared around the side of the house.

"And you're sure the front door was locked?" Jack questioned Ellery.

"Yes. It always sticks, and tonight was no different. It took me a couple of seconds to get it open."

Jack nodded. "Right. You opened the door, and then what?"

"I'd left the kitchen light on, but it was still pretty dark in the hallway, so if there was anything amiss, I didn't notice. Watson wanted to play, so I threw his weasel up the stairs a few times, and then I went into the kitchen." Ellery drew in a breath.

"And?"

"It was obvious someone had broken in. Every cupboard was open, every drawer was pulled out. I think he went through the fridge. There's stuff all over the floor."

Jack's expression grew even bleaker.

"I started to back up—I knew I should phone from outside—and I, er, fell over Watson."

"You..." Jack looked down at Watson, who wagged his tail.

"Then Watson started growling and barking, and I realized whoever had broken in was still there, still in the house, and at that moment the guy burst out of the pantry and charged right at us."

Jack swore quietly. "You should have got out of there the minute you realized someone had broken in."

"I *did*. Or tried to. Jack, I'm giving you the play-by-play exactly as it happened. The only thing I could have done differently was not fall over the dog."

"You could have installed a security system when we first talked about it three months ago."

Ellery's jaw dropped. "Seriously? You're going to bring this up *now*?"

"It seems pretty damned appropriate, given the circumstances." Jack was terse, his voice low.

Whereas Ellery? His "Jack, you know as well as I do that it's going to cost a fortune to install a security system at Captain's Seat!" had Officer Battye, who had been on approach, sharply tack port and steer a fresh course for the back of the house.

"Have you even bothered to get an estimate?" Jack asked, still quiet, still annoying as heck.

"Yes, I got an estimate back in May. And it's going to cost a freaking fortune. There are a million windows—"

"You could start by securing the perimeter. That would be something."

That would indeed be something. Something that would still cost a fortune, though yes, a smaller fortune.

Of course, the five-thousand-dollar check he had deposited that afternoon would go a long way toward securing this old barn. Ellery opened his mouth to say so, but it occurred to him that Jack might not be in the best possible frame of mind to hear how Ellery was earning that handsome fee.

"I'll bear it in mind."

"Do." Jack was curt. "In the meantime, were you able to get a good look at the intruder?"

Ellery struggled with his voice—and his feelings. He understood that Jack was worried for him. *He got it.* But he'd had an alarming—no, let's be honest, frightening experience—and a little sympathy would have been nice. At the least, a tactful pause before once again bringing up the sensitive topic of alarm systems would have been appreciated. Jack was acting like it was Ellery's *fault* his home had been broken into, and that wasn't logical or fair.

"I already told you. No."

"Unless you kept your eyes shut the whole time, you must have seen something."

Jack probably didn't *mean* to sound sarcastic. His tone was not sarcastic. But that warm hug he'd given Ellery sure felt like a long time ago.

"He was big," Ellery snapped.

"Big? That's it? That's the only thing you noticed?"

Was Jack was *looking* for a fight?

Ellery tried to match Jack's flat, impersonal tone. "Taller than either of us, though it's hard to be sure since I was flat on my back. Broad, muscular. *Burly.* That's the word. But he moved easily, like someone in good shape and used to physical activity. I think he might have had red hair, but then again, that could have been the mask he wore. It had two red wings sticking out like ears."

Jack opened his mouth but seemed unable to locate an appropriate response.

"I couldn't see his eye color or his face," Ellery tried to explain. "It happened really fast. There wasn't—"

"It always does."

Argh. Ellery said, "Great. So is that it?"

Jack looked taken aback. "No, that's not it. What are you talking about?"

"I'm tired. It's late. I don't want to stand here arguing all night."

"I'm sorry you think we're arguing. I'm sorry you've had an unpleasant experience. But we still need to finish this interview. The goal here is to catch this ass—your intruder so he doesn't come back."

Ellery opened his mouth, but they were interrupted by Officer Martin, who was made of sterner stuff than Officer Battye. "Chief, it looks like our guy got in through some unlocked doors on the back terrace."

It was hard to tell in the moonlight, but Jack seemed to change color.

"There weren't any unlocked doors," Ellery said.

Martin was still talking. "It doesn't look like he made it to the second floor, but the ground floor has been turned upside down."

"I'll be in to have a look," Jack said.

Ellery said, "The French doors were locked."

Martin sounded almost apologetic. "We couldn't see signs of a break-in, but maybe."

Jack turned to Ellery and said grimly, "You'll have to put together a list of everything that's missing. Assuming this was about theft and not something else."

Ellery let out a long shaky breath, nodded. Jack thought Ellery's stalker had broken into Captain's Seat, that tonight was a further escalation. Which made sense.

Though that explanation had not occurred to Ellery until now.

It should have. But for some reason he hadn't connected the break-in with his stalker. He'd assumed it might be connected to his sleuthing or that he'd walked in on another burglary. But how likely was that, given that the burglary ring that had plagued the island for much of the summer had been broken up?

No, Jack was likely right about this. Despite the warmth of the night, Ellery shivered.

"What about the intruder's vehicle?" Jack asked. "Did you get a glimpse of it? Did you pass any parked cars on the main road?"

"No. I never heard or saw any vehicles from the time we left Pirate's Cove."

Jack continued to ask what were probably pertinent questions, and Ellery did his best to answer.

"One thing about the mask he wore," Ellery said suddenly. "I think it was vintage. I don't think it's something you can just grab off a shelf. It looked like molded plastic, not vinyl."

Jack said thoughtfully, "That could be significant."

"I don't know how helpful it is, though. This guy has access to vintage costumes? Except, it's not like a Bozo mask is a theatrical costume. More like something kids would have worn for Halloween thirty years ago."

"Thirty? More like sixty. Do clowns figure in any of the Halloween movies you made?"

"*Clowns?* No. Ghosts, demons, witches. The last film had a gargoyle." Ellery shuddered at the recollection. The quality (all things being relative) of the *Happy Halloween! You're Dead!* films had deteriorated drastically with each installment. "Even if there had been any clowns involved, they wouldn't— couldn't—have been Bozo. The character is trademarked."

"How do you happen to know that?"

"One of my college roommates created a campus meet-up website, and he made a login graphic with Bozo. The Bozo estate filed a cease and desist."

Jack considered. "So the subject might be a collector? Or have access to a collector? Or he's a creepy stalker who just happens to love clowns?"

"I guess," Ellery said doubtfully. "I mean, this break-in could be completely unrelated to my stalker. It's not like we haven't had burglaries and break-ins before."

"That would be one hell of a coincidence."

"True. But." Coincidences did happen. They both had plenty of experience with that.

Jack said, "I don't like the fact that most nights you'd have been home when this guy broke in."

True. And that was not a happy thought.

"Maybe he knows my schedule. It doesn't vary much." Did knowledge of Ellery's comings and goings support Jack's theory that the break-in was tied to the threatening letters? Probably. Ellery said without much conviction, "But maybe he chose this house at random. Maybe it doesn't have anything to do with me."

"Maybe." Clearly, Jack wasn't buying it.

"Maybe he works during the day and this was the only time he had off."

That actually silenced Jack for a moment. But only a moment. "If someone is watching you, they know your schedule. You're out plenty on the weekends. They could have picked another night."

Was there maybe just the faintest edge in that *You're out plenty on the weekends*? Ellery wasn't sure. Jack knew Ellery occasionally went out with Robert Mane, but he'd never indicated that was a problem for him. Jack knew he had nothing to worry about where Ellery was concerned.

Ellery said neutrally, "I work Saturdays, and I'm not out that many evenings. Not lately. *You're* here a lot of nights. Maybe this was more about *your* schedule."

Oops. Should he not have said that in front of Officer Martin? Jack liked his private life kept private. But it wasn't like Jack—like either of them—was *hiding* their relationship. There were probably few people in Pirate's Cove who didn't at least have an inkling that he and Jack were seeing each other. Figuring out the perfect balance was tricky sometimes.

Jack didn't bat an eye, seeming to weigh Ellery's suggestion. "Yeah, maybe." He sighed, then said crisply, "Regardless. We'll get someone out here ASAP to dust for fingerprints."

Ellery nodded. He couldn't remember if the intruder had worn gloves or not. Brown rubber boots. Those he remembered. The boots and the Bozo mask.

"As for tonight..." Jack stopped short.

Well, this was awkward. For Jack, anyway. Especially with Officer Martin standing by, gazing up at the stars and trying not to listen.

Since they had started dating, Ellery had spent exactly one night at Jack's house. For whatever reason, Jack did not invite him to stay over. Their nights together were always spent at Captain's Seat. Which was mostly fine with Ellery—he liked sleeping in his own bed—but it would have been handy on game night or the nights he joined the Silver Sleuths Book Club to crash at Jack's.

It was that kind of thing, little things, really, that kept him from feeling completely secure in their relationship. Yet hands down, Jack was the most considerate, caring, and, even, candid boyfriend he'd ever had. He trusted Jack. But he didn't entirely trust Jack's *feelings*. Did that make sense?

Anyway, the problem tonight was that the chances of Ellery finding an available room anywhere in Pirate's Cove were slim to none. His options were sleeping in the Crow's Nest or sleeping in the middle of a crime scene, and both were equally unappealing.

Jack must have reached the same conclusion at the moment Ellery did, because without a word, he pulled out his keys, removed his house key from the ring, and handed it over.

"I'm not sure when I'll be home. I may have to wake you up."

"Yeah, no, that's fine. Thank you."

"Well, no, of *course*." There was a funny note in Jack's voice, a note of protest at whatever he thought Ellery might be thinking.

Ellery took the key and shoved it in his pocket, as though he could possibly hide it from Officer Martin's memory.

CHAPTER TEN

Why hadn't his stalker tried to kill him?

Not that Ellery was complaining, but that was the threat, right?

You. Will. Die.

Or words to that effect. But when the opportunity had arisen, the stalker had shot past Ellery and Watson as if fleeing for *his* life. Why wreck the house and not Ellery?

Again, not a complaint. Just a question. One of many. And all of them would have to go unanswered for now because Ellery was on automatic pilot by the time he arrived at Jack's.

He parked on the silent, sleeping street, went up the short brick walk, and let himself into the tidy beach cottage.

The cottage was dark and smelled as clean and airless as a tightly shut bottle of sanitizer. Ellery fumbled for the light switch. Watson, who had spent a lot more time at Jack's than Ellery, disappeared into the gloom. Ellery could hear him sniffing energetically around the living room, Watson reassuring himself that no cats had been in residence while he was away.

At last Ellery located the wall switch. Cheerful light illuminated a pleasant room with large windows facing the quiet street. The furniture looked like Jack had purchased the whole collection, everything from the lamps to throw pillows, from a showroom. It was solid, comfortable stuff, and gave absolutely no clue as to the homeowner's personality—beyond the fact that Jack liked the color blue.

Last time—well, the only time—he'd spent the night, there had been no pictures on the wall, no books anywhere, no framed photographs or knickknacks or souvenirs. That hadn't changed, which underscored that this was just a place where Jack slept. On duty or not, Jack's waking hours were mostly spent at the police station.

Until recently.

Recently, he had begun spending more time with Ellery, but still, PICO PD was Jack's real home.

Ellery went into the kitchen, found Watson's bowls neatly stacked on a shelf in Jack's mudroom. He filled one dish with water and sprinkled a little kibble into the other. He poured himself a glass of water and went to sit on the blue sofa in the blue living room.

This escalation in his stalker's behavior worried him. A lot.

It worried Jack too. That was obvious. It was one reason he'd been so short and snappish at the...the, gulp, crime scene.

Admittedly, Ellery was no expert, but it seemed like two threatening letters, spaced months apart, might reasonably be expected to be followed by more threatening letters spaced months apart. In fact, that was kind of what he'd been expecting. More letters. Or maybe phone calls, except phone calls could be traced much more easily, especially on such a little island.

Breaking into his home and wrecking the place was an unexpected and alarming move.

Much more threatening. Much more violent.

And yet, when the opportunity arose, no violence had been committed on Ellery—or even Watson, who had been doing his best to bite the intruder.

Was the goal simply to scare and harass? If so, mission accomplished. Ellery was feeling harassed, and he had definitely been scared.

He was less scared now, sitting in the somewhat sterile comfort of Jack's domicile, and that was a testament to his confidence in Jack.

But Jack was worried, no question.

Which meant Ellery was right to be worried as well.

The buzz of his phone on the nightstand woke Ellery.

It took him a confused moment to understand that he was in Jack's bed—minus Jack—and that it was two in the morning. He peered blearily at his phone's screen and saw the blue bubble of Jack's: Sorry. You'll have to open the front door.

No spare keys under garden gnomes for Jack. One key and only one key. One key, which Jack was confident he would never lose or never loan out. Which probably said something important about Jack. Something Ellery did not want to try to decipher.

He threw back the sheets, ignoring Watson's moan, and picked his way across the unfamiliar floor, through the living room, and opened the door.

Jack, bathed in a yellow glow of porch light, looked very tired and very grim.

Some of the grimness left his face at the sight of Ellery, hair on end and wearing nothing but his skulls-and-crossbones boxers.

"Sorry. Maybe I should think about—"

Ellery cut him off with a kiss, wrapping his arms around Jack's shoulders and hugging him hard.

After a surprised moment, Jack responded, arms clamping around Ellery, his mouth warm and hungry. When their lips parted, Jack murmured, "Well, ahoy there, Matey."

"Welcome aboard, Captain," Ellery said, and Jack chuckled.

"We're not going to get anything useful in the way of fingerprints," Jack told Ellery over their toast and coffee the next morning.

"I figured."

"That doesn't mean we're not going to find this guy. We are."

Jack's default was confidence. Both in himself and in good police work. Ellery hoped that confidence was well placed, but the Crow's Nest had a sizable True Crime section full of books where good police work had not saved the day.

He nodded noncommittally.

Jack swallowed a mouthful of coffee, studied Ellery, and put his mug down. "About last night. I'm sorry if I came off a little..."

Ellery tilted his head, waiting. He was smiling, but he did want to know what Jack thought of their interaction the night before.

Jack settled on, "Gruff..."

"Gruff?"

"It's only because—and I don't want to get into an argument over this because we've talked this out before and I respect your...your position."

Ellery raised his brows. "This sounds kind of ominous."

"No. Not at all. But I can't help feeling that, even though you've had some close calls, you still don't realize how quickly things can go really wrong. Drastically, deadly wrong."

Ellery resisted the impulse to instantly deny or dismiss Jack's criticism. That was the thing: it wasn't criticism so much as concern. He took a moment to form his reply.

"I don't feel that's really fair, especially when it comes to last night. I don't think I could have done anything different. Except falling over Watson. *That,* I could have handled differently. But this stalker started writing me months ago, before I ever had a thought of amateur sleuthing."

Jack also took a moment to respond. "That's true. You didn't bring this on yourself. You're a victim of someone else's…delusion. Or whatever it is. But you've known for months that someone feels they have a grudge against you, and you haven't really done anything to protect yourself."

"I had the locks changed at the Crow's Nest, which is all I could afford at the time. Captain's Seat is a whole other thing. There are at least eight points of entry on the ground floor—and that's not counting windows. I don't—didn't—have the money for that. But I do plan on putting a security system in. Which is something I wanted to talk to you about. Something came up yester—"

"I'm not only talking about security systems," Jack interrupted. "I'm talking about your-your…propensity for putting yourself into potentially dangerous situations."

Propensity? Jack was in a no-nonsense mood, for sure. He was definitely not going to be in a receptive frame of mind to hear Ellery's news about agreeing to help out Mrs. Wallace.

Ellery sighed—probably a little too long and a little too loudly because Jack reddened and said,

"Yeah, I know we've arg-*talked* about this a lot. A lot more than I'd like, believe me."

"I do believe you."

"See, there's that tone. That snippy tone. Which confirms for me that you don't take any of this seriously enough."

Ellery sucked in a sharp breath but managed to say quietly, "Okay, Jack—and I don't want to get into an argument over this with you *either* because I agree we've talked this out before and I also respect *your*—your position. And your experience." He paused. This part was awkward and liable to be painful, but he believed it was the truth. He said very carefully, "I think what happened to Hannah and…the baby colors your view. I think going through that terrible experience is why you feel everything is potentially dangerous, that everything is so…fragile."

Jack had been red, but now he was bone-white. His throat moved as he swallowed. He said in a stony voice, "Everything *is* fragile. You've lived a sheltered life if you think otherwise. Things can change in a heartbeat. A situation can go south before you know it."

"That's the cop talking."

Ellery was startled when Jack yelled, "You're damn right, it's the cop talking. The cop who's seen firsthand what can happen. Who's had to break *terrible* news to parents or wives or husbands. Who's had to try to explain stuff that doesn't make sense, that should never have happened."

Jack shoved his chair noisily back, rose, and went to the kitchen sink to stare out the little window.

Watson, who had been regarding their exchange uneasily, rose, putting his paws on Ellery's knees as though asking to be picked up. Ellery patted him automatically, still watching Jack. His heart thumped sickeningly. Jack was so angry. Angry but controlled. In a weird way, the control was more intimidating than the anger.

How had they got here? Five minutes ago, they'd been smiling and debating the merits of raspberry versus strawberry jam.

He said, "I'm sorry."

"I know you are." Jack was terse. He kept his back turned to Ellery.

And Ellery *was* sorry, but he still believed he was right. What happened with Hannah and the baby had to—and *obviously* had—affected Jack's understanding of the entire universe. But at the same time, Jack was also right. Jack's experience as a cop was something Ellery had no understanding of or insight into. Police officers saw the world in a different way than ordinary citizens. How could they not when they had to deal with the worst side of people day in and day out?

This was not the moment Ellery had been waiting for, but given the circumstances, he couldn't put off any longer telling Jack about his decision to help Mrs. Wallace.

"Jack, I have to tell you something. You're not going to like it."

Jack turned then. His face was still pale, but his blue eyes were hard as slate. "Go on."

Ellery had run over his mental script for this conversation a number of times, but now that the moment had come, he forgot his prepared remarks and blurted out, "I wanted to tell you earlier, but I didn't get the chance. I've agreed to help Odette Wallace find out who's trying to kill her."

Whatever Jack had expected to hear, it wasn't that. Something like relief flickered in his eyes, but whatever that emotion was, it was gone in an instant, to be replaced by another emotion that looked a lot closer to outrage.

"Are you freaking kidding me?" Jack demanded. Not that he said *freaking*, and though Ellery had heard and also used the word-that-was-not-freaking many times, he'd never heard it used with quite that scalp-prickling emphasis. Not from Jack.

"No. I'm not. But it's not what you think." Which had to be one of his dumber comments.

Jack surely agreed because he shot back, "Really? You're *not* helping her, or you are?"

"I am, but I'm not acting as her bodyguard."

Jack's jaw dropped. Not an expression Ellery had seen much, and in other circumstances, amusing. In these circumstances? No. Not at all. Jack sounded a little winded as he repeated, "Her *bodyguard*?"

"Mr. King, her lawyer—"

"I know who King is."

"—is hiring an actual bodyguard. I'm just—"

"You're just what? You're a private investigator now?"

Ellery had been interrogated by Jack once, but even when Jack had considered him a murder suspect, he hadn't used that tone of voice. It rattled Ellery. Jack's tone *and* the artic blast of his gaze. "No! Of course not. I'm just helping her out with her-her problem."

"Any problem that woman has is a problem of her own making. *Why* would you involve yourself in something like this?"

"She asked for my help."

Once again, Jack seemed at a loss for words. "How the hell would that happen? How would she know you even *exist*?"

That probably sounded ruder than intended, right?

"Apparently, Kezzie Harwood told her I'd helped figure out what happened when Brett was murdered."

"That's just *freaking* fantastic." Once again Jack did not say *freaking*. He was pretty irate, no question. "Did she actually *hire* you?"

Ellery faltered. "Well, yes, she did actually... hire me."

There was a dangerous gleam in Jack's eyes. "She's paying you, then? So you have a private investigator's license I'm unaware of? Or are you operating without a license?"

"Oh, come on, Jack," Ellery protested. "You know it's not like that. I'm not pretending to be a PI."

"No?"

"I'm acting as a-a consultant."

"So you're what…an armchair criminologist? What *exactly* are your qualifications for this job?"

Throughout their entire conversation, Ellery had been telling himself to keep cool, to listen and not react defensively, to look at the situation from Jack's point of view. But Jack knew damn well what Ellery's qualifications were. He'd even admitted to Ellery's mom that Ellery was good at puzzles and had been of use on a couple of cases. So, in Ellery's opinion, Jack was kind of being a jerk just to be a jerk. He wasn't letting Ellery really explain. He was simply drawing his own—worst—conclusions.

"You know what my qualifications are. I'm a-an amateur sleuth. Which is what Mrs. Wallace wants."

Jack looked ceilingward in that *God give me strength* way that was starting to feel too familiar. "For the love of—what does *that* tell you? She doesn't want or need professional assistance. This is an act she's putting on, and you fell for it."

"Why would she bother?"

"Are you aware that Odette Wallace murdered her husband?"

Funny thing. Hearing Jack say it, made it a lot more real. Ellery believed it. He believed the hardness in Jack's eyes. It was clear Jack knew things Ellery did not. Ellery believed Jack because Jack believed what he was saying.

But how much of Jack's certainty was based on Colby Wallace whispering in his ear?

Not a pleasant image, that.

Ellery said, "I know she was suspected and charged, but that the charges were dropped for lack of evidence."

"That's not exoneration. That means there wasn't enough evidence at the time to prove the case beyond a reasonable doubt in court. There's no question she did it."

"Clearly there's *some* question." That was probably his *snippy* voice, but by then Ellery didn't care.

"Not in the eyes of the investigating officers."

Ellery snorted. "You mean Chief Ballard? I already know what you think of Chief Ballard's police work, Jack."

"Ballard wasn't the investigating officer. Yesterday evening, I talked to the detective who handled the case, and I think he's right. I think she got away with murder."

It was a jolt to find out that Jack had gone so far as to check with the detective who had worked the case—and that the detective still believed Mrs. Wallace was guilty.

Not that detectives didn't sometimes get it wrong. Detective Lansing *still* probably believed Ellery was guilty of somebody's somewhere murder.

Even Jack sometimes got it wrong.

Ellery said stubbornly, "That doesn't mean someone isn't trying to harm her now."

Jack said impatiently, "No one's trying to harm her. There's no motive for anyone to harm Odette Wallace. She's trying to throw up a smokescreen."

Ellery retorted, "Your question back at you: why would she?"

"Because she knows the investigation into Wallace's death is going to be reopened and she's the prime suspect."

Ellery stared. "Wait. The case is being *reopened*?"

Jack nodded, his expression impassive.

"Since when?"

Jack said flatly, "Since I spoke to Colby Wallace yesterday and he convinced me to take another look."

CHAPTER ELEVEN

"**E**llery! I have to talk to you!"

Ellery, in the process of unlocking the front door to the Crow's Nest, turned to see Sandy Morita hurrying up the wooden walk toward him. Sandy owned the small art gallery next door, and lived upstairs with her young daughter Terry, who was Watson's regular babysitter.

Watson was wagging his tail as Sandy reached them. She was slim and graceful with waist-long black hair and, thanks to colored contacts, brilliant turquoise eyes. Though usually smiling and unruffled, that morning her expression was troubled.

"Hi there," Ellery said. "What's up?"

"I think someone tried to break in here last night."

"Into the Crow's Nest?"

Sandy nodded. "Someone was loitering in the walkway between the buildings, and I got the idea they were checking to see if there was a way in through one of the side windows. I didn't phone the police station because he—I think it was a he—ran off when I yelled at him. It could have been a kid, but…"

"It's not like there's a lot to attract kids in here." That was a sad statement, but true.

"No, and he didn't seem kid-sized."

"Did you get a good look at him?"

"Not a good look, no. It was after ten, and the walkway is dark. But his shadow was large. Man-sized, not boy-sized."

This was not good news. "Someone broke into Captain's Seat last night and was in the middle of ransacking the downstairs when Watson and I got home."

Sandy's eyes went wide. "Oh my gosh. Thank goodness you two are okay! What did he want?"

"I'm not sure he wanted anything except to wreck the place."

"But *why*?"

Ellery shrugged. "I guess somebody doesn't like me."

"Jeez. I guess not." Sandy patted his arm. "Well, *I* like you, and I'm glad you're okay. I'll be sure to keep an eye out. In fact, I'll go phone the station and report what I saw, for what it's worth."

"Thanks, Sandy."

Sandy nodded, gave Watson a quick pat, and sprinted back to the gallery.

Ellery finished unlocking the door and cautiously pushed it open. The bell chimed softly. The scent of old books and Murphy's Oil greeted him. Ellery let out a long breath, gazing in relief at the wooden floors warm and gleaming in the morning sunlight, the jewel-toned spines of row upon row of books filling the tall shelves, the muted rainbow of the ship's lanterns lining the back wall, and the antique oil portraits of sailing ships forever at sea, forever battling painted storms.

Everything was just as he had left it yesterday evening.

"Thank God," he murmured.

Watson trotted past Ellery, snatched up his green frog, and squeaked it in invitation.

"Maybe later," Ellery told him.

Could a puppy frown? Watson considered, dropped the frog, and picked up a fuchsia and orange Fuzzball instead. He squeaked it enticingly.

Ellery reluctantly laughed, managed to get the Fuzzball from Watson, and tossed it across the room. He watched absently as Watson bounded after the toy, which he proceeded to throw in the air.

Jack was right about one thing. Ellery needed to get serious about safety.

In fact, Jack had been right about a number of things. But he had been wrong about some things too. Things that were kind of fundamental. Ellery sighed. Unsurprisingly, he and Jack had not parted on good terms that morning.

Which was to say, they hadn't parted on *bad* terms, exactly.

They weren't out-and-out yelling at each other, so hey. Granted, they hadn't been speaking much at all, so... Maybe Jack had forgotten to kiss Ellery goodbye. More likely, he hadn't been in a kissing mood. Neither had Ellery, if he was honest. The fact that Colby Wallace could get Jack to open a closed homicide investigation bothered him. The fact that he and Jack were on opposite sides on this case, bothered him even more.

In fairness, they were often on opposite sides of a case. It just felt *more* opposite this time.

Learning from Sandy that his stalker had stopped by the Crow's Nest before heading out to Captain's Seat was just piling on more bad news.

If that guy had got in here and trashed the bookstore, it wouldn't merely be upsetting and worrying. Ellery couldn't afford to fund a lot of repairs or buy new inventory. Not being able to open for business would have practical, possibly even long-term consequences. The lucrative summer months were closing fast enough as it was.

Last night Ellery could have easily been, well, maybe not ruined, but his prospects of financially surviving the winter would have been seriously impaired, for sure.

No, Jack was right. Ellery needed to prioritize protecting himself and his livelihood.

He jumped as the brass bell on the front door jangled in alarm, but it was only Nora, struggling to shut the door against the stiff and sudden sea breeze.

"Storm's coming!" Nora called. She leaned against the door, slightly out of breath. "I was doing my best to get here early so we could discuss the case, but I ran into that garrulous old fool Elijah Murphy at the Brewhouse and just couldn't get away! Here you go." She handed over a thick manilla folder stuffed with what appeared to be printer copies of web pages.

"What's all this?"

"Everything I could find on Tristan Wallace's murder. I stayed up late last night, scouring the internet."

Ellery flipped through the folder. "This is…a lot."

"Yes. Don't worry. We've all got copies."

He asked warily, "We've all *who* got copies?" But really, why ask? He knew perfectly well who else was on the receiving end of Nora's internet sleuthing. He didn't need Nora's cheery, "The Silver Sleuths, of course!"

"Of course. Nora, you do remember that there's no proof Wallace was murdered. Officially, the death was ruled accidental."

"Initially," she corrected. "Later, the medical examiner's finding was changed to *undetermined*."

Or, in police-speak, To Be Continued.

"Okay, but our job isn't to solve the mystery of what happened to Tristan Wallace. It's to figure out who might want to harm Mrs. Wallace."

Watson brought his Fuzzball to Nora, who took it from him and hurled it with startling accuracy across the width of the store and through the office doorway.

Seriously? said the look Watson gave her before he loped after the toy.

"The solution to the first question will provide the answer to the second," Nora assured Ellery. "Now, what did you learn yesterday?"

"I don't know, Nora."

Nora looked surprised. "You don't know what you learned?"

"No, I mean, I don't know that we're doing the right thing by involving ourselves in this case. *Either* case. Jack is *really* unhappy about this."

"Oh, pshaw," Nora returned.

"That's easy for you to say."

Nora's blue gaze was shrewd. "Did you cash the check?"

Ellery nodded reluctantly. "I did, but I haven't spent it yet. I could give the money back to Mrs. Wallace."

"But why?" Nora seemed genuinely puzzled. "You need that money every bit as much today as you did yesterday."

"Because, for one thing, Jack thinks she *did* kill her husband."

Nora didn't miss a beat. "Does that mean it's open season on her?"

"No, of course not. But Jack also believes she's faking these supposed murder attempts."

Nora frowned. "But after all, she might very well be innocent. She might truly be in danger. What did you think of her story?"

Ellery thought back to that uncomfortable interview on Mrs. Wallace's yacht. "I'm not sure. It all sounded pretty unlikely." He proceeded to fill Nora in on the attempts on Odette Wallace's life as related to him by Mrs. Wallace and Mr. King.

Nora heard him out without interruption.

"I *think* she believes someone is trying to kill her," Ellery concluded doubtfully. "But honestly, she's difficult to read. Mr. King believes her, and that, more than anything, convinced me maybe she *is* in danger."

"Howard King." Nora's tone was thoughtful. "I remember him. He handled all the television interviews after the accident. I believe he and Wallace were college roommates. He always gave the impression his loyalty was to the family brand rather than any one family member."

"That may have changed along the way. I got the feeling he and Mrs. Wallace are personally involved."

"Ah-ha," Nora murmured. "So if she *did* commit murder, he might turn a blind eye?"

Ellery thought that over. "I'm not sure. He seems more like the Regretfully-I-Must-Do-My-Duty type to me. He dismissed the idea that Mrs. Wallace could commit murder, and he discouraged the idea that one of the Wallace kids might be involved."

"He's known them since they were children."

"Right. Which is what Mrs. Wallace said. Of course, they're not children anymore, and there's a lot of money involved—though I'm unclear about the details of who inherited what when, or how that might be relevant. King admitted the Wallace kids always hated their stepmother. He seemed to imply Wallace was to blame for that."

"I believe it. He was an awful little man. A tin-pot tyrant."

"King insists that Wallace killed himself."

"Because he was terminally ill," Nora observed, proving she had listened carefully to Ellery's accounting of the previous day's interview. "But I have to say, I can't imagine Wallace doing away with anything he prized as highly as himself."

"Not even to avoid the pain and suffering of a terminal illness?"

Nora said dryly, "The Wallaces of the world get all the pain medication they need when they need it. There wouldn't have been so much pain and suffering. There would be indignity, of course, and that would have been hard on his ego. Death is very hard on control freaks."

Ellery bit back a smile at Nora's prim *control freaks*, but he was serious when he said, "Anyway, getting back to my original point, I'm wondering if this time we've bitten off more than we can chew."

"How so?"

"There's a lot going on right now."

Nora smiled knowingly. "Naturally, Chief Carson is miffed, but he'll get over it."

Miffed? Had Nora seen the wintry look in Jack's eyes or heard that cold, clipped voice, she wouldn't have described him as *miffed.*

"I don't like arguing with Jack, but that's not what I mean. Someone broke into Captain's Seat last night and pretty much tore the place apart. And according to Sandy, they may have tried to break into the Crow's Nest earlier in the evening."

"What?" Nora stared. "But that's…"

"Enough to deal with." Ellery had never told anyone but Jack about the anonymous letters, so he didn't tell Nora he was afraid the sender of that hate mail had raised the stakes to breaking and entering.

"No, no. That can't be a coincidence."

"That's what I'm saying. We don't need this kind of trouble right now." Or ever.

Nora said impatiently, "Dearie, I don't believe this is anything to do with *our* case. This is something different."

Uh-oh. The last thing he wanted was the news he had a stalker to spread around the village. He tried to come up with a good alternate scenario, but it turned out Nora already had one.

She said eagerly, "Not thirty minutes ago, Elijah Murphy told me that someone broke into the *Fish-*

ful Thinkin' Sunday night and turned the boat upside down."

Ellery blinked. "What do you mean, *turned the boat upside down?*"

"It's only a turn of phrase, dearie. I don't mean *literally.*"

"No, of course not, but are you saying it was a burglary?"

"It's possible." Nora's tone seemed to dismiss that as unlikely. She eyed Ellery expectantly.

Why? What was he missing?

He asked slowly, "Was anything stolen?"

Nora shook her head. "According to Elijah, no."

The synapses in Ellery's brain began, belatedly, to snap, crackle, and pop. "You mean they were *searching* for something?"

Nora's eyes gleamed with approval. "It certainly sounds like it to me!"

A break-in at Captain's Seat, a break-in on the *Fishful Thinkin'*, and an attempted break-in at the Crow's Nest. Nora was right. How could this be a coincidence?

In fact, now that Ellery thought about it, maybe the chaos at Captain's Seat hadn't been willful destruction so much as ruthless exploration.

Was that the answer? Was someone looking for something?

What?

What possible thing could someone be looking for that might be on the *Fishful Thinkin'* as well as at the bookstore and Captain's Seat?

"Was anywhere else in the village broken into last night?" he asked.

"Not that I'm aware of." Nora added, "So far."

Ellery glanced at the clock. Just after nine. By eleven, Nora's numerous and varied sources would have reported in, and they'd probably have a definitive answer on that.

In the meantime, was there a common denominator between those three locations?

An obvious answer was Ellery. He had been to all three places within the last couple of days.

Was his stalker...

No. No, that made no sense. Ellery had been to plenty of other places too, including Jack's cottage, so it had to be more than that. No, this couldn't be about Ellery himself so much as something someone believed Ellery might have, or have had, in his possession.

But that didn't make sense either. No one in Pirate's Cove (or anywhere else) was going to mistake him for a drug smuggler or a jewel thief or a...what?

Assuming nowhere else in the village had been hit, this had to be about something that had been onboard the *Fishful Thinkin'*, but which someone now believed Ellery might be in possession of.

That something couldn't be the body or the diving suit because anyone paying the least bit of attention had to know the suit and remains had been taken straight to the Buck Island Med Center mortuary.

What, then?

A clue to whoever had killed the unknown diver?

Was Jack right about Ellery's reputation as an amateur sleuth coming back to haunt him?

But any and all clues would surely have gone with the body and would now be in the possession of PICO PD. Even the dumbest of criminals would *have* to assume that.

On the one hand, it was an enormous relief to think that maybe the break-in at Captain's Seat and attempted break-in at the Crow's Nest had nothing to do with his stalker. Ellery much preferred the idea of a murderer dumb enough to believe he could be in possession of some telltale clue, to the idea of a psycho stalker in a clown suit.

Not that he was *happy* about either scenario, but one felt more survivable than the other.

Nora, meanwhile, was busy with her own thoughts. "Did Sandy get a look at the person trying to break in?"

"Not a good look. It was late, and the walkway is dark."

"Yes. The town council needs to put some kind of lighting along these walkways." Nora considered, suggested, "Could this person have been Kingston?"

Ellery did a double take. "Could it have been *Kingston*?"

Nora nodded excitedly. "Is it possible?"

"No, it's not possible. Not if the person who broke into Captain's Seat was the same person trying to break into the Crow's Nest. That guy was three times the size of Kingston."

Nora looked disappointed. "That's a shame."

"Nora." Ellery shook his head. He'd have said more, but the door opened with a discordant peal of the bell as the wind blew in the first customers of the day.

CHAPTER TWELVE

"**R**obert's taking us on a tour of North Point lighthouse this afternoon." Ellery's mother neatly speared a bite of crab salad. "Why don't you pull rank and come along?"

Technically, Ellery was already pulling rank by sneaking in an early lunch with his parents at the Seacrest Inn's café.

"So it's *Robert* now?" he teased. Not that he was surprised. Robert and Talia had hit it off from their first meeting yesterday at this very table.

"He's very charming."

"He is." No question. Robert was very charming.

"Wonderful sense of humor."

"That too." Ellery always had a great time with Robert.

"And handsome."

Ellery turned to George. "Are you getting worried yet?"

George sighed heavily. "Very." He winked at Talia.

Talia grinned back. "George knows *exactly* where he stands."

"That's true." George, untroubled, took another bite of chicken and dumplings.

"Anyway, what's the point of owning your own business if you can't take the occasional day off?" Talia coaxed.

"I would, but we're really busy today." So busy that Ellery had ended up calling Kingston to ask if he could come in early. Their summery weather had turned unexpectedly cold, with wind out of the northwest shoving a forbidding wall of black clouds over the suddenly gray and choppy water. With a weather forecast promising heavy rain and possible thunderstorms, Race Week attendees were prowling the streets of Pirate's Cove, looking for other ways to amuse themselves. Some might even be desperate enough to resort to reading.

Talia made a face. "All right, but we're on for dinner?"

"Absolutely."

"Is Jack joining us?" George asked.

"No. Jack's working." He must have sounded more curt than he intended because George and Talia exchanged looks. Ellery softened it with, "Race Week means everyone at PICO PD works overtime."

"Well, I hope we get to see him again," George said. "I like him."

"Mm-hm." Talia sipped her wine.

Ellery gave George a grateful smile, though the thought of Jack weighed on his heart. Officer Martin had phoned before Ellery had left for lunch to *request the list of names Chief Carson had asked for yesterday.* Ellery was trying not to make too much of that, but he couldn't remember another time Jack had delegated talking to him to someone else.

Jack was not happy with him. No question there.

The last thing Ellery wanted was to fall out with Jack, but he also wasn't going to be bullied. Okay, *bullied* was too strong a word. But, as much as he respected Jack's opinion and cared about Jack's feelings, he wasn't going to be pressured into making decisions he wasn't comfortable with.

Except, he acknowledged ruefully, by Nora, apparently.

Anyway.

They had reached the should-we-shouldn't-we-do-dessert stage of their luncheon when Talia excused herself to, as she deadpanned, *powder her nose.*

As soon as she was out of earshot, Ellery turned to George and demanded, "Why doesn't she like Jack?"

"She does."

"No, she doesn't, and I don't get it because he's the opposite of everyone I ever dated, which you'd think would be a good thing."

George said patiently, "It's really not about Jack. It's about the fact that, for the first time in your lives, she can't read you. You're making life choices she can't predict and doesn't understand. Starting with packing up your entire life and moving to an island you'd never even visited before. It's not that she objects to your choices; she's just afraid she's losing you."

"She's not losing me. I'm not going anywhere—or at least, I'm not going anywhere else."

George smiled. "*I* know that. *You* know that. Even Talia knows that. Don't worry."

Ellery nodded. He wished he felt as sure as George. Talia always gave him a hard time about his boyfriends, but this was the first time he'd felt she was genuinely concerned.

Or maybe this was the first time he actually *cared* what she thought of his boyfriend?

"You know, I wasn't getting anywhere in New York. There wasn't a future there for me. I was just… drifting." That was the truth. When his acting career had stalled out, Ellery had coasted through a series of dead-end jobs.

George nodded. His eyes were kind.

Before moving to Pirate's Cove, Ellery had been *rudderless*, as they said on the island. Without drive or direction. Then Great-great-great-aunt Eudora had popped up out of nowhere with her crazy bequest, and suddenly Ellery had been in possession of a failing business and a falling-down home and a loudmouthed puppy, and he *loved* it. All of it.

He couldn't ever remember being this happy. Or this stressed. But mostly he was happy.

And that wasn't even counting solving mysteries or falling for Jack Carson.

"Don't worry, son." George smiled. "I know you both pretty well by now, and it's going to work out just fine."

Ellery smiled. He wasn't one-hundred-percent convinced, but as always, he felt better for talking things over with George.

* * * * *

Nora and Kingston were bickering when Ellery returned from lunch.

He had slipped in as a customer was leaving, so Nora and Kingston, who were standing behind the Hard-boiled and Noir shelves, weren't aware he had returned.

Ellery knelt to greet Watson, listening uneasily as he petted the dog.

"There's really no comparison," Kingston was saying. "Chandler was a poet. Even his routine descriptions of the most mundane things are startlingly, breathtakingly original."

"Which is my very point," Nora returned. "No one reads hard-boiled detective fiction for breathtakingly original descriptions. Metaphors and figurative language are all very well, but Hammett is the master of spare and direct storytelling, which is what the hard-boiled reader wants."

"*Yikes,*" Ellery murmured. Watson tipped his head from side to side as though trying to pick up a far-off radio frequency, which was pretty much how Ellery felt.

He'd known the situation between Nora and Kingston wasn't good, but Chandler v. Hammett? *Really?*

Ellery had never been anyone's boss before. Frankly, he had never *wanted* to be anyone's boss before. But this was his bookstore. He was the person in charge. As much as he did not like conflict, part of his job description was figuring out how to resolve conflict when it arose.

Or, he could just take Watson for a walk?

Kingston, sounding like a man smiling through gritted teeth, said, "That's not what *this* hard-boiled reader wants."

"Perhaps you don't *know* what you want," Nora replied sweetly.

Oh-kay. That was more than enough. Ellery hopped up, gave the bell on the door a push, and called, "I'm back!"

Kingston and Nora came out from opposite ends of the Hard-boiled section like prize fighters breaking at the end of a bout.

"Oh good, you're back!" Nora chirped.

"Did you have a nice lunch?" Kingston didn't exactly chirp, but there was a guilty sprightliness to his tone.

"Yes I am, and yes I did," Ellery began, but broke off as Nora handed him a note with a phone number.

"Mason Wallace?" He glanced up in surprise. "Really?"

Nora's eyes were bright with excitement, but she said casually, "He'd like to speak to you as soon as possible."

This was an unexpected turn of events. (Also great timing.)

"Then let's see what Mason Wallace has to say," Ellery replied.

Mason Wallace apparently had a lot to say but preferred to say it in person rather than over the phone, so a few minutes later Ellery found himself in a small motor boat crossing the very choppy gray-green water to a small, sleek yacht with the tasteful moniker *Wet Dreams*.

It was raining as Ellery clambered on board the yacht. His host was not there to greet him, but he was escorted across the slippery deck and down a slippery flight of stairs to a small blue lounge where four people—two men and two women—sat waiting for him.

Mrs. Wallace had described Mason as *a little schnook*, so Ellery was surprised when the man who rose to greet him introduced himself as Mason Wallace.

Mason looked a lot like his older brother, Colby: tall, blond, and handsome. Or at least like Colby had looked from a distance. But then Ellery had already guessed that Mrs. Wallace was what was known in the book biz as *an unreliable narrator.*

Brief introductions were made. The willowy, elegant woman in white jeans and oatmeal sweater was introduced as Vanessa. The equally elegant dark-haired man beside her—in complementary white sweater and stone-colored jeans—was Ralph. A petite, twentysomething blonde in shorts, halter top, and goose bumps was Bailey.

Ellery nodded politely to the wall of well-groomed, expressionless faces.

"You can sit down there." Mason pointed to one of the bolted-down, navy-blue banquettes. He had clearly been drinking all day, but coffee not alcohol. He buzzed with caffeine and antagonism.

Ellery sat where indicated and studied his hosts with polite inquiry. He had no idea what to expect from this crew, but he was sure it would be interesting.

Mason said, "Howard feels it's to our advantage to convince you that none of us have any interest in laying a hand on Odette."

"I wouldn't go that far," Ralph muttered, then grimaced. "Sorry."

"It's the most ridiculous thing I've ever heard," Vanessa said. "And considering the source, that's saying something!"

"She's just saying it to get attention." That was Bailey. She was wearing rings on every finger, so

Ellery wasn't clear if she was Mason's wife or girlfriend or personal assistant with benefits.

"But Mr. King witnessed the attempts on Mrs. Wallace's life," Ellery said. "He believes someone's trying to harm her."

"Other people have close calls and don't instantly imagine someone's trying to kill them," Mason said.

"This wasn't just—someone spiked her wine with antifreeze. They cut her brake lines."

If Ellery thought they'd be impressed by that, he thought wrong.

Ralph said—again in that growly undervoice, "I think good old Howard is starting to lose it."

Admittedly, Ellery didn't know Mr. King well, but he didn't seem like someone who was remotely *losing it.*

"She seduced him. Like she did Daddy." Vanessa glared at Ellery as though Mrs. Wallace seducing Howard King was specifically his fault.

"I can guarantee you, Howard doesn't think any of us had anything to do with trying to *murder* Odette," Mason said. "He knows it's ridiculous, which is why he wanted us to talk to you."

The rain thundered down overhead. The lounge windows (not portholes by any stretch of imagination) were as steamy as if curtains had been drawn.

"Okay," said Ellery. "So if it's not any of you, who do you think might want your stepmother out of the way?"

"*If* it's not us?" Mason repeated in disbelief.

Ellery corrected, "Assuming it's not you, who—"

"Do you have a pen and paper?" Bailey asked.

"Oh for—! She's *making this up,*" Vanessa said. "The whole thing's fabricated."

"What would be the point of making it up?" Ellery asked. "What would she gain from that?"

Bailey gave a *duh!* kind of laugh.

"But seriously," Ellery said. "What is there for her to gain by pretending someone's trying to kill her? And how could she convince Mr. King to go along with it?"

"Who knows?" Mason sounded impatient. "That isn't our job. Our job is to set you straight."

Ellery deadpanned, "And don't think I don't appreciate it."

Mason's eyes narrowed.

Vanessa sat up ramrod straight and snapped, "*Do* you? Just who do you think you are, Mr. Page? That woman murdered our father. Do you have *any* clue how offensive this is?"

"The *only* reason we're talking to you is because Howard asked us to." That was Mason again.

"I realize that," Ellery said. "I realize this is probably painful—"

"*Probably?*" Vanessa's voice shot up a couple of octaves.

"—but on the off chance that someone *is* trying to kill Odette—"

"Good!" Vanessa snapped. "I hope they succeed!"

Ellery wasn't sure what to say.

"She doesn't mean that," Ralph said quickly.

Judging by Vanessa's set expression, Ellery couldn't help thinking Vanessa probably meant every word.

"What exactly did she do to you?" he asked.

"You mean, besides kill our father?" Mason retorted.

"I see. You all got along great before that?" Ellery wasn't being sarcastic—okay, maybe a little bit. He wasn't crazy about Odette, but these four? He was liking them less and less by the minute.

Bailey said, "You don't know what it's like to have someone come in and try to take your mom's place."

"Actually..."

"Bailey," Mason interrupted irritably. "It's a lot more than—it wasn't anything to do with *Mom*. Odette's a gold digger. She targeted our father like he was a bull's-eye on a dartboard. When she met Dad, she was already engaged to Petey Windersnickle. But she dropped him like a hot...a hot..."

"Windersnickle?" Ellery couldn't help it.

"Tomato." Ralph said it with stern finality.

"Because Tristan Wallace was a lot richer and a lot more important." Mason shook his head in disgust. "She made our father's life *hell*. They fought twenty-four seven."

"That must have made it difficult to run his empire."

"You're damn right it did!"

Vanessa put in, "She tried to turn our father against us. *And* she had affairs. A *lot* of affairs. Which is another reason I can't fathom why Howard would fall for that *wah-wah-someone's-trying-to-kill-me!* routine."

Ellery tried to sift through that flood of…information? Maybe not information so much as special delivery verbal junk mail? "Is it possible someone she had an affair with might want to get back at her?"

"I can't imagine anyone would care enough about her," Vanessa answered.

So which was it? Odette was a femme fatale, or something Vanessa might scrape off her Dior sneakers?

"They did fire the pool boy," Bailey said suddenly.

The other three stared at her. "That's true," Mason said thoughtfully. "Maybe the pool boy did it."

Or maybe the butler did it. One thing for sure, Ellery was not getting anything useful from this bunch. The only thing he'd learned was that all four of them truly did hate Odette. Maybe enough to kill her, maybe not, but for sure none of them would shed tears at her funeral.

He made one last try to glean something helpful. "What about your brother Colby? Is it possible he might want Odette out of the way?"

Vanessa laughed.

"*Colby?*" Mason snorted. "You don't know Colby."

"Well, no. I don't know any of you. That's the point of this meeting."

Ralph said grimly, "Take it from me: if Colby wanted Odette dead, Odette would already be dead."

CHAPTER THIRTEEN

Ellery had still not heard from Jack when he returned to the Crow's Nest from dinner with his parents.

If he and Jack hadn't argued that morning, Ellery would have put the radio silence down to Race Week. As it was, well, it was hard not to take it personally. Granted, Ellery could always show initiative and phone Jack.

He seriously considered it while rifling through his file cabinet, looking for the quote he'd obtained back in May on a security system for the bookshop. Making the first move was surely the bigger-man thing to do. The problem was, he'd had a lot of experience getting slapped down by Jack, and he just didn't have the heart for it that night. Jack wasn't unkind, but he sure was efficient in handing out rejection.

Instead, Ellery phoned the security systems company, which turned out to be closed for the day. He left a message, and then he set about putting together the Potential Enemies list Jack had requested.

It was not an easy thing to do. He felt silly—and petty—trying to recall everyone who had ever seemed less than charmed by him. Having lived most of his adult life in New York, he was used to abrupt or brusque interactions. Jack was from California, where *Please, Thank you, Excuse me*, and *Have a Nice Day* were part of the native language. So Ellery was unlikely to register what Jack might consider a potentially hostile exchange.

In fact, the only people Ellery felt comfortable putting on his Potential Enemies list were those who might reasonably blame him (at least partially) for police interviews, legal fines, or actual incarceration. Those people *or* their nearest and dearest.

Surprisingly, even within that limited scope, Ellery's list turned out to be longer than he'd expected. He studied the column of names unhappily.

His cell phone rang. Jack's photo—taken the first time they'd gone diving—popped up.

Ellery grabbed his phone, warning himself to play it cool, and said cautiously, "Hi."

"Hi." Jack's tone was neutral. "I wanted to let you know we're all done at Captain's Seat."

Translation: *You can sleep in your own bed tonight.*

Ellery said crisply, "Great."

"It would be helpful if you could put together that list of anything missing ASAP."

Not an unreasonable request, but Ellery resented…well, maybe what he resented was that this was Jack's only reason for calling.

"Yep. I'll add it to my list of all the other lists you want."

The line was silent. Ellery folded his lips on his natural inclination to fill the void with pointless chatter. Jack had already made it clear this wasn't a social call.

Still. He didn't like arguing. In fact, Ellery's heart was banging so loudly in his ears, he almost didn't hear Jack's eventual, brusque, "Good."

You're making this worse.

Was he, though? Because other than Jack himself phoning to let Ellery know he could return home, Jack wasn't exactly reaching out to him. Nope. He was pointedly all business.

Fair enough.

"Was that it?" Ellery had to harden his voice to keep it from wavering, so he probably sounded more unfriendly than he intended.

There was another of those funny silences.

"That was it," Jack said pleasantly. "Have a good evening." He hung up.

Ellery thumbed the Home Screen button, depressed by the knowledge that if he and Jack hadn't actually been fighting before, they probably were now.

Membership in the Silver Sleuths Book Club did not change much week to week.

Maybe that was simply due to lack of interest, but Ellery suspected it was more about the fact that somewhere along the line the Silver Sleuths had transformed from bookshop book club to private social club.

Which was fine, hopefully, though unlikely to do much to bolster the Crow's Nest loyal customer base.

Less fine—even downright worrying, occasionally—was the club's preoccupation with crime. Not fictional crime. Real crime. Specifically, murder. More specifically, murders that took place on Buck Island.

That was not to say the Silver Sleuths had not been helpful to Ellery in his past sleuthing efforts. They were certainly doing their best to be helpful that Tuesday evening as they read through their copies of Nora's painstakingly compiled dossier on Tristan Wallace's watery demise.

"There's a typo page nine, paragraph eight, first sentence, dear," Hermione Nelson remarked, dusting powdered sugar from her copy.

"The typo is the webpage author's, dear," Nora retorted.

Edna Clarence chimed in, "Odette's name is spelled incorrectly multiple times in the *Newport News* article."

"You'll have to take that up with the *Newport News*, dear."

And so went the background soundtrack for the first thirty minutes.

The facts of the case were pretty sketchy. Sketchy as in scant, not sketchy as in suspicious. At least as far as Ellery could tell. Nearly a decade ago, coincidentally (?), during Race Week, Tristan Wallace had taken his superyacht, the *Siren Song*, for an evening cruise and never returned. Though Wallace's three adult children were participating in Race Week on their own yachts, no was alarmed when Wallace did not return to harbor on Buck Island.

(Ellery made a mental note to determine why Odette had not gone with Wallace on his evening cruise.)

Three days later, the *Siren Song* washed up not far from Port Judith in Newport, RI, around 1:15 a.m., with its navigation lights on and engines still running. Sea Tow, the company hired by Newport authorities to tow the boat, reported that the vessel appeared seaworthy with no detectable mechanical malfunction. There was no sign of Wallace or any other passenger on board. Authorities on ATVs searched up and down the coast but found no sign of Wallace. The Coast Guard commenced a search at sea. The search proved unsuccessful and was eventually abandoned.

Two months later, a nude male body washed up at the Surfer's End of Sachuest Beach. The Middletown Police Detective Division and the state Medical Examiner's office processed the scene, concluding there did not appear to be any suspicious circumstances surrounding the death. Days later, the body was identified by Mason Wallace and Howard King as that of Tristan Wallace.

Maybe Wallace had been a man who liked to come and go as he pleased, but it seemed like nobody had cared very much when he disappeared. He'd been missing for three days, and neither his family nor friends seemed to notice until the *Siren Song* was found, and then the only person who had given statements or talked to the media was Wallace's lawyer, Howard King.

That was the first red flag in Ellery's opinion.

The second red flag was the quick dismissal by the police and ME of possible suspicious circumstances in Wallace's death. To start with, how sure could anyone be, after a body had been in the water for two months, that there hadn't been foul play? Sure, certain things could be ruled out, like a bullet hole in the skull or blade marks on a rib cage, but there were plenty of other fatal things that could be done to someone—how about just shoving them overboard?—that couldn't be so easily ruled out.

Not to be ghoulish, but after two months in the water, how much of the victim had even been left to examine?

Ellery shuddered, and Stanley pointed a finger at him, cackling. "Someone's walking over your grave!"

Nice. He muttered, "I wish they'd wait till I'm in it," and the others laughed merrily.

Which led to Ellery's third red flag: identification of the body by Mason Wallace and Howard King. Presumably the identification had been mostly based on dental records or DNA or a silver shin bone (Ellery had noticed silver shin bones seemed to figure a lot in vintage PI novels). It couldn't have come down to Mason and King walking into a morgue somewhere and recognizing a gold watch and a wedding ring.

This was where it would have been helpful to be able to talk to Jack.

"What did Tristan Wallace look like?" Ellery asked.

"It's in your file, dearie," Nora said.

"Pages four, six, ten, and…" Jane Smith licked her index finger, flicking rapidly through the print-outs.

"Got it." Ellery studied what was surely the facsimile of a corporate portrait.

Wallace had been well into his sixties when he died, and he had still been handsome, but there was an unattractive hardness to his face. His thin mouth was curved in a miserly little smile like he charged for it by the tooth. His dark eyes were small and narrow and cold.

Hard to imagine kissing that mouth or searching those eyes for understanding.

Wallace didn't look well, so that might be part of it. His shoulders looked slightly bowed, his neck sort of shrunken. Maybe he had already been ill at the time the photograph was taken. Maybe he was in pain or knew he didn't have long to live.

"Was he a big man?" Ellery asked. Wallace's offspring all looked like they were descended from disgruntled fashion models. Wallace was no fashion model.

"No," Stanley said. "He was a runt."

"Small in mind and body," Nora agreed.

"Yes! He was a meanspirited little man," agreed Hermione. "He had a reputation for not paying his contractors."

"Stiffing them," Stanley said bluntly. "He was famous for never tipping, or, if he was forced to pay, shortchanging. I think he was sued by at least three businesses on the island."

"The Shandys sued him," Edna said. "I remember that. It got very nasty. Threats were made on both sides."

"Wallace had no shortage of enemies, both personal and professional," Nora agreed. "But it's hard to see why any of those people would hold a grudge against Odette."

"Do you think maybe we should focus more on Odette's background?" Ellery asked. "If investigation begins with victimology, isn't Odette our victim?"

This got scowls all around.

"You're assuming these two cases are connected, but maybe they're not," Ellery said.

Nora said, "They must be."

"Why must they be?"

"Well…" Nora frowned, considering. "Hm. I suppose you're right. We're assuming Odette has been targeted by one of the Wallace offspring. But it's possible she's made enemies all on her own."

"If it's one of the Wallace children, it'll be Mason," Hermione said wisely. "I have it on good authority Wallace was planning to cut him from his will."

"I'm sure that's wrong," Nora said. "I'm sure it was Colby who was going to be disinherited."

Ellery said, "Maybe Wallace was the kind of person who was always threatening to fire people or cut people out of his will?"

Hermione and Nora beamed at him.

"I don't doubt he was!" Hermione said.

Jane Smith said suddenly, "I heard Odette Wallace has hired Tackle Shandy to be her bodyguard."

"Wherever did you hear that?" Nora looked astounded, though probably more by being scooped by Jane than by Jane's news.

Jane shrugged. "I heard it from Nicole who heard it from Greta. June Shandy works for Greta at her shop."

Hermione sniffed. "Such a ridiculous name. Greta's *Gourmandery*. There's no such word! What was wrong with Greta's Gourmet Goodies?"

"Just a second," Ellery said. "One of the Shandys is now working for Odette Wallace?"

He might as well have been talking to himself.

"Where *is* Nicole these days?" Edna asked Nora.

Nora shook her head and gave a meaningful look at Stanley, who bristled and said, "Don't look at me. It's not my fault the woman can't take a joke."

Nicole Ferris had been a charter member of the Silver Sleuths, but there had been some falling out between her and Mr. Starling at a meeting where Ellery had not been present. The details remained shrouded in secret and powdered sugar.

"Tackle is out of prison, then?" Hermione asked Jane. "I had no idea."

"It seems so. I admit I was surprised to hear it. But he served five years."

"It must be the fastest five years on record."

"Not for Tackle, I bet," Stanley interjected.

Against his will, Ellery found himself sucked into the riptide of local gossip. "What was he in for?"

"Involuntary manslaughter," Nora informed him. "It really wasn't his fault, though."

"Maritime law is so confusing," agreed Edna.

Ellery sat back in his chair. "I think maybe we're getting off-track."

Nora, Edna, Hermione, Stanley, and Jane looked at him with surprise.

"Do you, dearie?" Nora asked. She glanced at her cohorts, smiled kindly at Ellery. "Where do you feel we should focus our attention?"

She was humoring him, but whatever.

Ellery said, "Maybe we should look at who has the most to gain by getting rid of Odette."

"That's easy," Nora said. "They all do. All the Wallace children."

"Do we know that for a fact?"

The Silver Sleuths nodded or made sounds of assent.

"Odette inherits three quarters of Tristan Wallace's estate. The remainder of Wallace's fortune is split among his three children."

"Even a quarter of that fortune is a considerable amount of money," Stanley said.

"But why settle for a third of a quarter when you can have…whatever it would be with Odette out of the way," Jane said.

Nora said, "The main reason Odette came under suspicion—aside from the younger Wallaces pointing the finger at her—was that Wallace was planning to divorce her. That's a matter of record. The paperwork was started, but nothing had yet been filed."

Now there was a bit of news.

"But wouldn't it be easier for Wallace's kids to sue for a bigger piece of the estate than commit murder?" Ellery objected. "Murder is risky."

"And so messy," Stanley agreed with the world weariness of a professional hitman.

"They tried, didn't they?" Hermione looked to Nora for confirmation. "Based on Wallace's stated intent to divorce her."

Nora nodded. "Perhaps if the divorce papers had actually been filed, they'd have gained more traction. But they weren't. And her lawyers successfully argued that Wallace could very well have changed his mind again, since it wasn't the first time he'd threatened to divorce her."

"Nice guy." Ellery pondered for a moment. "Okay. Vanessa, Mason, and Colby have the strongest motive for getting rid of Odette. Why would they wait ten years?"

"Oh, that's easy," Edna said. "It's the tenth-year anniversary."

Happy Anniversary! You're Dead. It had a familiar ring to it.

Nora, seeing his puzzlement, explained, "Wallace's fortune has been in trust for the last decade. On the tenth anniversary of his death, the money is to be released without constraint to his heirs. I expect someone has been hoping for ten years a solution might present itself. Had Odette remarried, for instance, she would have lost her share of the estate."

"What a you-know-what," Ellery muttered.

"Yes, he was. And he delighted in being one. Anyway, once Odette inherits, she can pretty much do as she likes with the bulk of the Wallace fortune. She could even go so far as to liquidate her stocks in the Wallace holding companies, which I'm sure the others would view as a complete disaster."

"I bet it's the first thing she does," Jane said. "I would."

Finally, things were beginning to make sense.

Ellery said, "So there *is* a time factor here. What's the actual date of the tenth anniversary of Wallace's death?"

You'd think that was a simple enough question, but it sparked a surprisingly (or maybe not surprisingly, all things considered) heated debate over whether the powers that be had been right or wrong in ultimately deciding the anniversary of Wallace's death was to fall on the date he had sailed out of Pirate's Cove rather than the date his body had been discovered on Sachuest Beach.

At last Ellery cut in. "To make a short story long, *when* is the drop-dead date for Odette to, er, drop dead?"

Nora broke off arguing with Stanley to reply, "Saturday, dearie. She needs to be dead by this Saturday."

CHAPTER FOURTEEN

No point in pretending he wasn't a little nervous about returning to Captain's Seat.

After all, what was to prevent last night's intruder from returning tonight for another look for whatever he had been searching for?

And he had definitely been searching. Ellery felt sick as he stood in the kitchen doorway, studying the carpet of canned goods, cooking utensils, trivets, and spoiled food scattered across the kitchen floor. He stared at the pulled out and emptied drawers, and swallowed—he'd never before realized how many knives he had. He took in the wide-open cupboards.

"I don't get it. What does he want?"

Watson, one paw delicately raised, leaned over to cautiously sniff an unopened can of uncooked pumpkin. He drew back, looking up in wonder at Ellery.

Ellery shook his head. "Beats me."

Interestingly, only the deep cupboard drawers had been hauled out. The narrow drawers, like the drawer for silverware, were untouched. So whatever someone was looking for, it was too big to fit in a cookie jar or an ice-cube tray.

Ugh. All that wasted food. A week's worth of food.

And yet, once again, it seemed to Ellery that the destruction had been incidental and not the point. Dishes and glasses had been shoved to the side of cupboard shelves, things had fallen to smash on the floor, but the shelves had not been swept clean. Food had been cleared from the refrigerator shelves, but the refrigerator had been closed afterward. The bottles and jars on the door were still intact.

Weird.

He was more convinced than ever that this was not the work of his stalker. Was it terrifying to know that someone had broken in, searched through his things, destroyed his property, and could come back and do it all again?

Yes.

But terrorizing him seemed more and more likely a repercussion and not the goal.

Whereas for his stalker, terror was the goal.

Ellery sighed. It had been a long, long day, and more than anything he longed to crawl into bed, pull the covers over his head, and forget his troubles for a few hours. Instead...

"Let's get at least some of this cleaned up," he told Watson. "I don't want to wake up to the smell of rotting celery."

Watson, of course, thought midnight house-cleaning was a terrific new game, and he did his best to bite the broom and pounce on the dustpan as Ellery set about clearing out the worst of the damage.

Even with Watson's, er, help, it took longer than Ellery had hoped, and the kitchen was still going to need a good scrubbing before it felt like his own again.

He tried to remind himself that it could have been a lot worse—which was certainly true—but he was still feeling depressed as he tied shut the last trash bag. Then he made the mistake of checking the rest of the downstairs, and felt a whole heck of a lot worse.

Nearly every book in Great-great-great-aunt Eudora's library had been pulled from the shelves and tossed to the floor. Hundred and hundreds of books were strewn everywhere.

Ellery felt almost light-headed staring up at the towering, white, shockingly empty bookshelves. Some of the shelves had probably not been touched in hundreds of years. Numbly, he gazed at burial mounds of faded and dusty books. Yellowed pages and leather book boards had torn off during the ransacking and were strewn around the room like fallen leaves.

He swore quietly, flicked off the wall switch, and closed the double doors.

Watson seemed to sense his distress, because he stood on his hind legs, whining to be picked up.

Ellery scooped the pup up, burying his face in Watson's soft black fur. "It's okay, buddy," he said muffledly, unsure if it was actually Watson he was trying to reassure.

But yeah, it *was* okay. Neither he nor Watson had been harmed in the break-in. Everything else was just…stuff.

He jumped at the sound of his cell phone ringing from the kitchen. After one was pretty late for phone calls, so this was either more bad news or…

Watson began to wriggle wildly. Ellery dropped him, sprinted back to the kitchen, picked up his phone, and his spirits rose. Yes, it was Jack.

Which, he warned himself, could be more bad news.

The message on his phone screen read: I know it's late but

Talk about a cliff-hanger.

??? typed Ellery.

He nearly dropped his phone as the doorbell chimed, the heavy sound rolling slowly, solemnly through the halls and corridors of Captain's Seat.

Watson raced down the front hall, yapping his excitement.

Arf! Arf! Arf!

As Ellery hurried to unlock the door, his own excitement was tinged with wariness. If someone had broken into the Crow's Nest, Jack would have led with that, and it would have been a phone call, not a text, so this was not that.

What this *was*, was unclear.

Which was not like Jack. Cryptic predawn texts were not Jack's style.

No wonder Ellery was anxious as he slid the bolt and opened the heavy door.

Jack, his eyes dark and hollow, his face an ominous yellow in the porchlight, stared back at him.

"I saw the lights were still on," he said.

Watson, doing his best impersonation of a kangaroo, jumped up and down between them.

"And you just happened to be in the neighborhood?"

ARF!

Jack's mouth curved in a humorless smile. "No. I was hoping you'd still be up. Can we talk?"

ARF!

Ellery swallowed, bracing himself. *Here it comes.* "Yeah, of course," he said quietly, and turned to lead the way.

Jack's hand locked on his shoulder, Ellery glanced back in surprise, read the longing in Jack's eyes, and the next instant they were in each other's arms—Watson yipping in alarm as he narrowly scooted out from between them.

When Ellery could breathe again, he gasped, "I thought we were in a fight."

"We are in a fight," Jack muttered. "But I miss you too much to stay away." His warm mouth found Ellery's once more.

When they reluctantly parted lips a second time, Ellery whispered, "I miss you too. And I don't want to fight with you."

Jack sighed, rested his forehead against Ellery's. "Then please let's not."

Later, in bed upstairs, the whisper of summer rain filling the silence between them, Jack said abruptly, "I saw you at the Salty Dog having dinner with your parents and Robert Mane tonight."

Startled, Ellery opened his eyes. Jack's smile was self-mocking in the soft lamplight.

It was warm and comfortable like this, resting in each other's arms beneath the satirical gaze of Captain Horatio Page's portrait, but though they'd spent a pleasant and reassuring twenty or so minutes, talking was one thing they hadn't done.

Ellery laughed. "No, you didn't. Robert was there for less than ten minutes before his pager went off and he had to head over to the Med Center."

Jack's brows drew together.

"The only reason he was there at all was because he and my parents had been out touring the North Point lighthouse. I had no idea he was going to be there. Where were you? I never saw you."

"I left."

"You…left?"

Jack was still smiling that odd, crooked smile. "I had the idea that eating at the Salty Dog was not going to be good for my digestion."

Ellery thought that over. He didn't mind Jack being a little jealous. Never again did he want to feel like he was the only one invested in a relationship. But he also wanted Jack's trust. Needed it, really. You couldn't have real intimacy with someone you didn't trust.

He said quietly, "You know, I'm honestly not sure what's going on between us, Jack. It's not like we haven't been on opposite sides before."

"We've never been on opposite sides like this," Jack said.

"Okay, but why does it have to be *like this*? What is it that's so different this time?"

Jack didn't answer.

"We talked about this just a couple of weeks ago," Ellery persisted. "I thought we'd come to an understanding. You even admitted to my mom Sunday night that my—that I've been helpful a few times."

"I know."

"You said that amateur sleuthing was becoming a growing trend that law enforcement had to take into consideration, and that your main concern was that I wasn't always careful enough, and I promised to be more careful—which I'm being."

"Are you?" Jack cocked an eyebrow.

"Yes! I am. I'm being careful." Ellery frowned. "That's not what this is about."

"No." Jack sighed. "You're right."

He left it there, gazing darkly off into something—the future?—that only he could see.

"Well, you're kind of scaring me," Ellery said after a moment. "We're fighting, and I'm not even clear what it's over."

"We're not fighting. *Fighting*'s the wrong word."

"Call it what you want. We're not getting along, that's for sure."

Jack's index finger teasingly traveled down the little tracks of cartilage and vertebrae to Ellery's tailbone. "For sure, for sure?"

Ellery's smile was reluctant. "Not fair, Jack."

Jack gave another of those sighs. "I just have to work through some things."

"Oh no. No you don't." Ellery sat up, surprising Jack and earning one of those human-like grumbles from Watson, who had been curled on his other side. "You're angry with me—"

"No," Jack said firmly. "I'm *not* angry with you."

If only it didn't sound like he was trying to convince himself.

"Fine. But you're not happy with me. Which we've got to work out together. Or it won't get worked out." How Ellery knew that, he wasn't sure, because he was actually pretty terrible about talking through relationship stuff (just ask Todd), but he could feel it in his heart. Feel that if they didn't get this ironed out, slowly but surely Jack would draw away.

Jack regarded him for a moment, said finally, "When we talked about this before, about amateur sleuthing, you kept insisting that you were being drawn into these cases, that you didn't want to be involved in these mysteries, but you kept getting pulled in because of friendships or loyalties or bad luck."

"That's true. I did say that." The light began to dawn for Ellery. "It— At the time—"

"At the time it was true. Yes. And after everything that happened with Juliet Blackwell, my takeaway, rightly or wrongly, was that you probably wouldn't continue getting involved in these local mysteries. Or at least, it wouldn't be a regular thing."

Ellery was silent because he had kind of said as much. Jack wasn't wrong.

Jack continued in that careful, grave tone, "And see, the thing is, I never wanted to date a fellow cop. In fact, I made the decision early on that I didn't want to be involved with another member of law enforcement. One cop per family." Jack's smile was wry.

"Okay, but I'm not a cop. I'll never be a cop."

"Right. But..."

"This is a one-time-only deal, and I honest to God wish I hadn't agreed to it." Ellery stopped as Jack squeezed his hand.

"The problem is, I foresee us having this exact conversation, the I-wish-I-hadn't-agreed-to-it conversation, many, many times in the future. And maybe you're right. Maybe some of this does have to do with what happened to Hannah and... Bad things happen. We never think they're going to happen to us, but they can, and they do. Even when you're careful, even when you don't take unnecessary chances, even when you don't go looking for trouble."

"Jack…" There was no point trying to finish it because even if Ellery's throat hadn't clamped shut like a vise, Jack was still struggling through his explanation.

"And so I also foresee being worried about what you're up to, being afraid for your safety as a regular part of my life, and…" Jack drew a sharp breath, but then didn't finish his thought.

"You don't want that," Ellery managed to get the words out, his voice cracking right down the middle, along with his heart.

"I *don't* want that," Jack said honestly. "But as much as I don't want that, I don't want to lose *this* even more." He raised Ellery's hand and kissed it.

Such a courtly, old-world gesture. Ellery's eyes stung. He nodded, not even remotely reassured.

Jack seemed to see everything Ellery would have liked to hide, because he said gently, "Hey, I couldn't even go a night feeling like we were…feeling that distance between us."

"If I promise—"

Jack stopped him, smiling. "You don't have to promise anything. You're not doing anything wrong. Well, unless you're planning to operate as a PI without a business license."

"Funny," Ellery said thickly.

"No, I mean it. It's my problem, not yours. Which is why I said I needed to work this out on my own."

Are you going to be able to?

But Ellery didn't ask. Jack couldn't make that guarantee any more than Ellery could guarantee he wouldn't be involved in any more mysteries. Neither of them could foresee the future.

Instead, he nodded, said, "Where do we go from here?"

"To sleep. We both need it." Jack reached over, snapped off the lamp, and tugged Ellery down.

Ellery rested his head on Jack's chest and closed his eyes. He listened to the *thump* of Jack's heart, the *shush* of rain against the window, the *ticktock* of the old clock on the mantel.

CHAPTER FIFTEEN

"**H**ow do you know Colby Wallace?" Ellery asked Jack over breakfast.

Truthfully, it wasn't much of a breakfast. With the unpredictability of a cyclone, the intruder had left the tray of eggs intact, but Ellery's milk, bread, and bacon had all ended up on the floor. Ellery had done the best he could with the eggs, club soda, a bit of green onion, and two slightly stale English muffins he'd discovered at the back of the fridge.

Jack's cell had already rung three times with Race Week "emergencies," so he had been a bit distracted over the course of the meal, but now Ellery had his full attention.

"We used to run together. Back in the day." Jack's tone was suspiciously casual. Plus, it was such an un-Jack-sounding comment.

"You were friends? When was that?"

"When I was in college." Jack seemed to consider. "Yeah, we were friends. Friendly, for sure."

Ellery grinned. "How friendly?"

Jack's laugh was a little self-conscious. "Very friendly for a while. We liked a lot of the same things. Boats, diving, drinking... This was before I fell in love with Hannah, obviously."

"Obvi." Ellery was still grinning, but honestly, it was a little bit of a surprise. Not the diving and drinking and being a college kid. The other thing. The *dot-dot-dot*. And yet, he'd sort of guessed there was something like this between Jack and Colby. Kind of a space-time continuum kind of thing. The first time he'd seen them together he'd picked up on it, that hard-to-describe quality of intimacy. Two people for whom personal distance did not apply.

"He's someone you trust?"

Jack's brows shot up. "You'd have to define the circumstances. Rowdy was always wild as hell. Which was fun. Until it wasn't."

"But you believe him about Odette Wallace murdering her husband?"

Jack tilted his head, as though trying to get a better angle on what Ellery was asking. "Anyone who asks me to take another look at the suspicious death of a family member is going to get my attention, but there's got to be something there. In this case, I think there is."

"And you think it points to Odette?"

"I do. Yeah."

"Like?"

Jack seemed to weigh how much he was going to share. He drained his coffee cup, set it on the table.

"Here's the problem for your client. She argued publicly with Wallace several times over the course of the week. On the day Wallace disappeared, he told her in front of witnesses—"

"What witnesses?"

"Witnesses who were not members of his family."

"Okay."

"Wallace told Odette he was divorcing her. According to witnesses, she responded by threatening to kill him first. She has no alibi for the night in question."

"But if she wasn't on the boat with Wallace, she had to be somewhere on the island."

"She had a room booked at the Seacrest Inn, but she can't prove and no one could verify if she was actually in there or not. It was Race Week, so there were a lot of comings and goings. According to the maid, the bed wasn't slept in."

"Maybe she didn't go to bed," Ellery objected.

Jack nodded. "She claimed she sat up all night, smoking and thinking about her marriage."

"Which could be true. It's a circumstantial case."

"Yes. But it's a strong set of circumstances. If Odette Wallace wasn't extremely wealthy and able to hire the best criminal lawyers, I think this would have gone to trial and she'd have been convicted."

"*Great,*" Ellery murmured.

Jack studied him, and sighed. "But here's the problem for my side. Wallace's body had been in the water too long to be able to prove his death was anything but a drowning. He was terminally ill. And he was adamant about sailing alone that evening. There's no indication Mrs. Wallace went with him. In fact, it's pretty unlikely. So how did she get on the boat to do away with him? How exactly did she manage to kill him and leave no sign of violence? And how did she get back to shore?"

"One thing for sure. She'd have to have an accomplice."

"She would."

Ellery thought it over. "She and Howard King seem pretty tight."

Jack's expression grew quizzical, as if he wondered whether Ellery noticed he was arguing against his own client. "King was looked at—as were Wallace's daughter and sons. The animosity between the Wallace children and their stepmother seems as genuine as it gets. And at the time, King was engaged to a rich and sporty socialite by the name of Tansy Wallingford. Plus, he had, by all accounts, a pretty cushy job in the Wallace organization. It's hard to see why he would endanger all that to get rid of Wallace, when he seemed to be one of the only people on the planet Wallace actually got along with."

"Good point."

"That doesn't mean he couldn't have been involved, but there were no red flags."

"And what about Wallace's kids? Not working with Odette, but working on their own behalf."

Jack's smile acknowledged Ellery's point. "All of them had, at various times, complicated relationships with their father. Wallace was a difficult guy."

That's right. Jack would have some insight into the kind of father Wallace had been because of his former relationship with Colby.

"Did they all have alibis?"

"That's a fair question. Vanessa and Mason are each other's alibi. Colby's alibi is problematic. He claims to have been bar-hopping most of the night. He was in the Salty Dog for a while, but then he moved on to the Deep Dive, and at that point no one can verify his whereabouts."

"The Deep Dive, huh?"

Jack nodded.

"So really, none of them has much more of an alibi than Odette."

"Arguable."

"Yep. Which is why I'm arguing."

Jack grinned. "And as much as I would love to stay and keep arguing with you, duty calls." He rose, bent to kiss Ellery—then kissed him again—and was gone.

Unsurprisingly, Ellery was late to work.

Not drastically late, maybe twenty minutes or so, but even so, there looked to be a line in front of the cash register. His hopes rose. But at second glance, he realized his mistake. The Race Week crowd had not discovered a burning need for the newest Andrew

Mayne thriller. Instead, the Silver Sleuths seemed to be holding an impromptu club meeting in the Crow's Nest.

Nora's voice was slightly raised, and not one of them even glanced around at the chime of the front door bell.

"But that's wrong," she protested. "We never had an exhibit like that."

"But we did," Stanley insisted.

Nora looked baffled.

"Morning, folks," Ellery called, unsnapping Watson from his halter.

Not so much as a wave of acknowledgment. Something was sure up.

Nora said, "I think I would know!"

"I saw it with my own eyes."

Watson, tail wagging, trotted up to Mrs. Nelson. Mrs. Nelson was known to carry Skippy double peanut butter bites in the depths of her voluminous purse, and no amount of discouragement could keep her from sneaking one or two to the pup. She automatically passed one to him, without turning from the discussion.

"Everything all right?" Ellery asked, joining the crowd at the front desk.

"Of course, dearie," Nora greeted him distractedly. "When was this?" she demanded of Stanley.

"That last day. Right before we locked the warehouse doors. I'd left my sunglasses inside, and I went back for them. I remember walking down the rows of colonial costumes and Niantic artifacts, and in the very back corner, I saw the diving suit, propped up, large as life. It gave me quite a turn, standing there in the shadows. It almost looked alive. I'm not likely to forget that now, am I?"

"No," Nora agreed reluctantly.

It dawned on Ellery what they were talking about. "Are you guys saying you think the diving suit Jack and I found belonged to the Historical Society?"

"*Yes,*" chorused Stanley, Hermione, Edna, and Jane.

"*No,*" Nora said with equal vehemence. "We never had a vintage diving suit in our collection. We had a diving helmet of that period donated by the Shandy family. That's it. Believe me, we'd have *loved* to have something like a complete deep-diving suit."

"I believe you," Ellery said. "But two people saw the suit inside the warehouse before the building was locked up for how many years?"

"Who's this other person who claims to have seen the suit?" Nora demanded.

"Cap Murphy."

"Elijah said that?"

"When Jack and I brought the suit up, he said it was similar to the one the Historical Society had. So it seems to me, the suit *was* in there."

"It's certainly not in there now," Nora said.

"Right, which means, whoever put the suit in, took the suit out again."

And not for any benign purpose.

Nora must have drawn the same conclusion because it was the only time Ellery had seen her look genuinely at a loss. "I…suppose so."

"Was the helmet fastened on the suit?" Ellery asked Stanley.

Stanley nodded eagerly. "Yes. The suit was complete with helmet and hoses. I assumed there was a mannequin inside because it—the suit, that is—was holding a collection bag and spear gun. I almost thought I could see a face behind the mask grill."

Jane Smith audibly gulped.

"*Stanley,*" Nora said weakly.

Stanley murmured, "Vernon Shandy."

Ellery took in the circle of horrified expressions and realized what they were thinking.

"Hold up," he said. "There couldn't have been a body in the suit. Not at that time. Think of the, well, smell. And think of how rigor mortis works. A body that had been there for more than a day probably couldn't hold a spear gun and a collection bag or stand upright. There most likely *was* a mannequin in the suit."

The Silver Sleuths glanced at each other and began to laugh. Mrs. Nelson let out a long sigh of relief. "He's right. We're behaving like ninnies."

Nora said, "That means someone must have brought that suit to the warehouse and hid it among our exhibits when we were packing up the museum."

Ellery nodded. "That seems like a reasonable theory to me."

Edna said, "D-Does that mean a-a member of the Historical Society...?"

"No! Certainly not." Nora was adamant, though her eyes were frightened. "That's impossible."

Funny how Nora believed every citizen in Pirate's Cove capable of murder *except* the members of her precious Historical Society.

"I guess we have to ask ourselves two questions: First, who on this island might have had a complete historical diving dress in their possession. Second, who on this island would have had a good reason for getting rid of what you'd think would be a valuable family heirloom."

"Hiding it in the Historical Society's inventory was brilliant," Hermione remarked. "The only person likely to remember the society didn't possess such an item is Nora, and for all this person knew, Nora might never have had reason to open that warehouse again."

Hermione was probably right, but Nora swallowed hard at that idea. Ellery patted her shoulder. "That was just one of their mistakes, right?"

Nora nodded. She said with a shade of her old authority, "The truth is, any number of our oldest families might have historical diving apparatus in their basements or attics."

Stanley hooted his derision at this idea. "*Might*, sure, but we all know which of our oldest families is most likely to have something like that in their possession. The same family that *might* have an urgent reason for unloading a valuable family heirloom."

"The Shandys." Ellery was not asking a question.

The others nodded.

"And we all know what that reason would have been," Stanley added.

Once again, the Silver Sleuths nodded in solemn agreement.

Once again, Ellery gave voice to what the others were thinking. "Someone planned on hiding Vernon Shandy's body in that suit."

CHAPTER SIXTEEN

"Christopher Holmes will be on a book tour in December," Nora announced.

Ellery mumbled, "Mm-hm."

"It's his first tour in nearly a decade."

Ellery glanced away from his computer, where he'd been scouring the internet (in between the distractions posed by celebrity deaths and political scandals) for information on Colby Wallace. He stared blankly at Nora. "Who?"

"Christopher Holmes."

"Never heard of him."

Nora's expression grew patient. "He writes the Miss Butterwith series."

Ellery snorted. "He writes a series about a syrup bottle? And I thought that Ice Fishing series was idiotic."

Nora had had a rough morning, and her sigh was a little heavy. "No, dearie. Miss Butter*with*. She's a botanist. I thought the series had been dropped, but apparently, it's been renewed. In fact, there's going to be a new Christmas story this year."

"Really? That's nice," Ellery said indifferently, glancing back at his computer screen. Was Jamie Lee Curtis *really* coming back for another *Halloween* movie?

Nora was nothing if not persistent. "Since Mr. Holmes will be in New England, the publicity team at Wheaton & Woodhouse wants to know if we'd like to schedule him for a signing."

"He wants to come *here*? Won't any other bookstores let him sign?"

Nora didn't bother denying it was an odd choice.

"In December no less?"

"The island is very beautiful in December. Quiet and quaint and Christmassy."

"He must crazy."

"Probably."

"Well, I mean, if he *wants* to come, okay," Ellery said reluctantly.

Nora murmured, "I'll let them know how thrilled we are." She turned to depart Ellery's office, brushing away a little strand of cobweb that had floated down from the ceiling.

She looked upward, Ellery followed her gaze—and they both gasped.

A large square panel in the ceiling was slightly askew, creating a sliver-sized opening into what appeared to be a black void.

"Nora?"

"I see it."

"Is that the door to the attic?" Ellery was pretty sure he already knew the answer.

"It…it must be."

"He got in here through the attic!" Ellery jumped up and went to stand under the hatch. He peered up, not that he could see anything through that sinister crack. "I didn't even realize we *had* an attic."

"All these old buildings have attics." Nora spoke automatically. She met Ellery's gaze, her gray eyes wide with worry.

"That's why he didn't go back to Captain's Seat or try to break in here again. He already got in."

"N-n…not necessarily."

Nora was trying to reassure both herself and Ellery, but Ellery was certain. "Yes. He did. I'd have noticed that opening in the ceiling if it had been like that for months. And now that I'm looking around, I can tell someone was in here."

Which was true, but also hard to explain because the office always looked like it had been ransacked.

"Really?" Nora glanced around doubtfully. "What did he take?"

"Who the heck knows! Felix's two-week-old tuna fish? Libby's high school soccer team hoodie? You people are always tossing stuff in here when you don't know what else to do with it." Ellery couldn't help the note of asperity that crept into his voice. It was kind of aggravating the way everyone used his office as a junk room.

Nora looked defensive but didn't try to deny it. She said instead, "But what could he be after? The rare-books case is untouched."

She didn't even bother to mention the cash register, and *rare-books case* was a bit of a misnomer. They currently didn't have any books worth more than fifty bucks or so in the glass case.

"I know. It doesn't make any sense. But I'm *sure* someone was in here."

"You would know, dearie." Nora began to poke around the boxes of books.

Ellery went to the file cabinets, also searching for proof someone had been in his office.

"At Captain's Seat, it looked like he was trying to find something, but it wasn't an organized search."

"*Ah-ha!*" Nora exclaimed. "That's because *this* is not the mark of an organized mind." She pointed to the dusty outline of a boot print stamped across the closed flaps of one of the cardboard boxes.

It didn't get more real than that.

Ellery joined her, and they studied the print in stunned silence. Here was the definitive proof that someone with large feet and larger determination had broken into the bookshop.

"Do you think he found what he was looking for?" Nora asked.

Ellery shook his head. "No idea. Part of me wants to think so."

Nora made a sound of disapproval at this poor-spirited attitude. She said thoughtfully, "If we keep this to ourselves, we might be able to figure a way to set a trap..."

Ellery stared at her in alarm. "No way."

"But dearie, *think*. This is the perfect opportunity—"

Ellery backed away. "Nope. No way. Not this time. I'm phoning Jack!"

That, however, turned out to be easier said than done.

Jack was in a meeting, and when he did finally return Ellery's phone call, he sounded uncharacteristically harassed.

"Hey, I'm sorry. Can we talk later? I'm literally walking out the door to meet with the Harbor Master."

"Well..."

"Is it an emergency?"

"Not at this point. I think someone broke into the bookshop."

"*What?*"

"It looks like whoever tried to break in the other night, actually did end up getting in through the attic."

"Wait. Stop. What do you mean *whoever tried to break in the other night*? Are you talking about Captain's Seat or the Crow's Nest?"

"I'm talking about the Crow's Nest. Maybe Sandy didn't report it?"

"Maybe Sandy didn't report *what*?" Jack demanded. "Ell, I don't know what you're talking about."

So then Ellery—who Jack had seemingly just nicknamed Ell?—had to explain about Sandy believing she saw someone trying to get into the Crow's Nest. That outraged Jack on so many levels that he had to verify then and there whether Sandy had, in fact, bothered to report the alleged attempted break-in.

Ellery waited, listening to the on-hold music until Jack returned and informed him that yes, Sandy had reported the alleged attempted break-in, but since the alleged attempted break-in had been thwarted and since PICO PD was already dealing with one heart attack, two purse snatchings, three drunken fights, and seventeen lost, missing, or stolen cell phones, the hapless officer manning the phones—new to the island and unaware that the bookstore in question belonged to the Chief of Police's boyfriend—had made a judgment call.

"That's not a mistake he'll make again," Jack said grimly.

Ellery, momentarily distracted by the sound of raised voices from the sales floor, frowned, listening, then realized Jack had stopped speaking.

"I'm not sure relaying the call to a patrol would have made any difference," Ellery admitted. "By the time Sandy reported it, my burglar could have come and gone."

"Or not. I'll get a team over there as soon as I can. At the very least, we need to make sure there's no continued access through the attic."

Yeah, the idea of an intruder dropping down ninja-style into Ellery's office at any time of day or night was disquieting. "I appreciate that. Thank you." It was probably a bit like locking the barn door after the horse had fled, but still.

Loud and clear, Nora's voice drifted through the open door of Ellery's office. "The Sea Horse tavern was owned by Ethan Cleverbridge, and he was most certainly *not* Canadian."

Kingston's reply was quieter but every bit as adamant.

"Well, you're wrong," Nora shot back.

"Ellery?" Jack asked.

Ellery snapped back to awareness. "I'm here."

"Any idea what he was after?"

"No. But I do have possible information on the diving suit the body we found on the *Roussillon* was wearing."

Jack cut in. "That's great, but it's going to have to wait. I'll talk to you— *Oh*. Hell. One other thing. You'll probably get a call from Rowdy."

"From..." Ellery wasn't sure he'd heard correctly.

"Colby Wallace. I told him he should talk to you."

"Did you? That's…" Not what he'd expected, for sure.

"I just want you to hear him out. Ultimately we all want the same thing."

Did they, though? Ultimately, Ellery wanted Odette not to be murdered so he could in good conscience keep his fee. (Well, and also because *of course* he didn't want anyone to be murdered.) Whereas Colby, ultimately, wanted Odette in prison for murdering his father. What Jack wanted was anyone's guess.

These were not the same things.

It seemed Jack was learning how to read Ellery's silences because he said, "You want to interview him anyway, right? This is your chance."

Ellery cooed, "And to think you did it all for *me*."

Jack laughed. "In the long run, yeah. In the short term, I'm doing it for me."

"Mm-hm. Okay. I'll talk to him."

"Thank you. I'm sorry, but I really do have to go…"

"I know."

"But I'll talk to you tonight."

"Tonight? Okay. Great."

Jack added, "Meantime, *please* try to stay out of trouble."

"You know, it's not like I sent out invitations to all the burglars in town." As the words left Ellery's mouth, he had the funniest inkling he'd just hit on something.

BURGLARS. Eight letters for sixty-one points.

But was the intruder a burglar?

Jack, sounding only half joking, said, "Are you sure?" and hung up.

Ellery made a face, rose from his desk, and went to the door of his office.

"In 1750, colonists still considered themselves citizens of England," Nora's voice floated from the west side of the sales floor.

Ellery groaned inwardly.

From the east, Kingston returned, "Not if they were born in Acadia."

Watson, sitting in the middle of the front aisle, turned his head side to side as though watching a game of ping-pong. He wagged his tail at Ellery as though to say, Now *that's* entertainment!

"Which Ethan Cleverbridge was *not*," Nora said.

"I assure you, he *was*," Kingston replied in that same determined-not-to-show-his-irritation tone. "This is something I've researched extensively."

"Then I would have to question your sources."

"As I would have to question *yours*!"

Who on God's green earth was Ethan Cleverbridge? Some obscure crime writer from the 1750s that only these two would consider worth going to war over?

"Excuse me," Ellery called. "What the—"

He broke off as Nora came charging out from behind the Romantic Suspense aisle like a slightly windblown Valkyrie in sensible shoes. It was doubtful she even noticed Ellery hovering in the doorway, trying to decide whether to take shelter.

"*My source*," she cried, "is the impeccably researched, beautifully written, and...not badly illustrated *Ghosts of Buck Island*." She actually brandished a tattered copy of the book.

Kingston, who cannoned out of the Supernatural/Paranormal Mystery section, seemed to have at last reached his breaking point. His hair stood up like a cockatiel's crest, and his bow tie was crooked. He shouted, "There's a revised edition!"

"There most certainly is not!"

"There most certainly is!"

"I ought to know," Nora shouted back. "*I* am K.K. Peabody's greatest fan!"

Kingston goggled at her. Ellery hoped he wasn't about to keel over in an apoplectic fit. Even Nora looked slightly alarmed.

At last Kingston sputtered, "But *I* am K.K. Peabody!

CHAPTER SEVENTEEN

"**Y**ou couldn't have known," Ellery tried to comfort Nora.

Nora dabbed her eyes, muttering, "His name's right on the book cover."

"*I* never noticed who wrote *Ghosts of Buck Island.*"

She sniffed, inconsolable. "You read the book, what? Once? I've read it hundreds of times. I don't know why I didn't connect K.K. Peabody with...that man. His photo's right there on the cover flap."

"Come on, Nora. That photo's forty years old. I barely recognized Kingston even after I knew it was him."

That wasn't exactly true. Kingston had, of course, changed over the decades, but he did still look like himself.

Nora moaned, "I've made a complete fool of myself."

Kinda. Sorta.

"Oh well. What's a little paranoia and suspicion between friends?" Ellery teased gently. "At least there weren't any customers in the shop."

"Yes, there were," she gloomily contradicted. "They took shelter when we started our…our discussion." She gave another of those little moans. "It's probably all over the village by now."

It probably was, so Ellery didn't bother to deny it.

"*Oh damn.*" Nora gave her eyes another wipe. "Why didn't he tell us? He should have told us!" her voice rose indignantly.

Ellery shook his head. "It's not like Kingston writes for a living. He said it's just a hobby. He taught high school for twenty-three years."

Nora sighed mournfully. "It's such a wonderful book too. I'd never have thought *he* wrote it. Now he's ruined it for me."

"It's the same book, Nora."

"No." She mimicked bitterly, "*There's a revised edition!*"

Ellery managed to keep a straight face. "You have to admit, he was pretty nice about it. All things considered."

Nora closed her eyes in anguish.

It was true, though. In the initial shock of finding herself in the wrong, Nora had actually stammered out a stricken apology, which Kingston had shakily assured her was *quite* unnecessary, before asking Ellery if he might step out for some fresh air.

He asked curiously, "Why *were* you so sure he was a bad guy?"

She shook her head. "I don't know. I knew he looked familiar and..."

"And?"

"I suppose I was a little threatened."

"Threatened? By Kingston?"

Nora opened her eyes and made a face. "After all, how many know-it-all old codgers do you need wandering about the place?"

Ellery opened his mouth, but she muttered, "I know it's silly, but I was afraid..." She vigorously blew her nose. "This job means so much to me."

"It sure can't be the paycheck." Ellery studied her with rueful affection. "Seriously. If I had to get rid of someone, Nora, it wouldn't be you."

That drew a watery smile. "I know. Holmes has to have his Watson."

"Definitely not what I meant."

Nora's gaze was troubled. "He's going to quit."

"Maybe not. I hope not."

She said shakily, "I-I should probably resign."

"What? Heck no, you should not resign." Ellery's cell phone rang. He didn't recognize the number, but he had an inkling as to who this must be. He rose. "Hang on. I have to take this."

Nora nodded without interest, still brooding.

Ellery moved away, answering his phone with a crisp, "This is Ellery."

A pleasant male voice replied, "Hi, Ellery. This is Colby Wallace. Jack Carson suggested you and I should talk."

"Sure. When and where?"

"How about now?" Colby said. "I'm over at the Salty Dog."

Ellery had been expecting to be dragged out to another yacht for yet another demonstration of wealth and privilege, so this was actually a relief.

"I'll be there in five minutes."

Colby replied, "I'll be waiting."

* * * * *

Colby was seated at Jack's usual table. He waved a hand in greeting when Ellery walked through the pub door, so at some point Ellery had been pointed out to him. By Jack? Or, more likely, by someone in the Wallace orbit?

Ellery nodded in reply, making his way through the crowded tables. Off-season, the pub would have been nearly empty at this time of day, but during the summer months, it was always a challenge to find an empty table.

Colby rose, shook hands with a firm grip. "Ellery."

"Colby."

No question, Colby Wallace was a good-looking guy. Like Mason and Vanessa, he was tall and fair. He had blue eyes and a jawline most superheroes would envy. Unlike Mason and Vanessa, he was dressed like someone who actually mucked around on boats. He wore Levi's and a gray sweatshirt with a Corona bottle logo. Unless you paid attention to things like manicures and expensive haircuts, nothing about him indicated he was a rich man.

"Call me Rowdy, everyone does."

Yeah, not Ellery. Ellery pulled out a chair and sat down across from Row—er—Colby, who inspected him with open curiosity.

"What'll you have to drink?" Rowdy was drinking what looked like whiskey.

"Narragansett Lager," Ellery told Frankie as she reached their table.

"And I'll have another of these," Rowdy told her. Frankie gave him an it's-your-hangover look, and departed. Rowdy leaned forward on his elbows, his blue eyes bright with speculation.

"Thanks for talking to me, Ellery."

"Sure. It's..." My pleasure? Probably not. Though Ellery had definitely wanted to talk to the remaining Wallace sibling.

"I guess you and Jack are pretty tight?"

Ellery raised a brow. "Is that according to Jack?"

Rowdy's smile was unexpectedly engaging. "It is, yeah."

That caught Ellery off-guard. What did that mean? Jack was so private. Maybe Colby had hit on him, and Jack had declined? Or maybe Jack wanted Colby to know why Ellery was an okay guy to talk to?

"We had some times, me and Jack." Rowdy shook his head at what must have been some colorful memories. "I couldn't believe it when he told me he was going to settle down and become a cop."

As tempting as it was to pursue this angle in Jack's past, Ellery forced himself back to business.

"Jack seems to think you've got compelling reason for believing Odette killed your father."

"I guess that's a matter of opinion. How much is she paying you, if you don't mind my asking?"

Ellery waited until Frankie poured his beer and once again sped away, before quoting the number, and Rowdy looked genuinely startled. "That's surprising. Odette's pretty tightfisted. Maybe she *is* scared."

Maybe scared, but more indignant, now that Ellery considered it. Still, in a way, the indignation was as convincing as fear.

"Mr. King believes the attempts on your stepmother's life are serious."

"Which is *really* hard to believe," Rowdy said. "Howie's no fool. Well, except about women. But I thought he had Odette's number a long time ago."

"What *is* Odette's number?" Ellery inquired. He was expecting to hear something like 1-800-EVL-ST-PMUM.

Rowdy smiled faintly. "Believe it or not, I didn't have anything against Odette until she had my old man knocked off. And I don't completely blame her for that. He could be a real pill."

Rowdy did not say *pill*, of course. Probably no one nowadays said *pill*.

"Is it possible your father committed suicide?"

"No."

Mr. King thought otherwise, but Mr. King had also insisted Ellery sign that NDA. Ellery circumnavigated carefully, "He was terminally ill, wasn't he? That's public record. Why are you so sure he didn't kill himself?"

"Plain and simple: he wasn't the suicidal type. He thought he was going to beat his illness." Rowdy gave another of those brief smiles. "He figured he could buy his way out of that too."

That was a fresh perspective, and believable given what Ellery knew of Tristan Wallace.

"Okay, but it seems like some people disagree."

Rowdy's smile was cynical. "You mean Howie?"

"King knew your father from way back. Knew him for longer than you did. Why do you think he—"

"Because that's the kind of thing Howie would do. He'd want to spare everybody the fuss and muss of a long, fatal illness." Rowdy gave a short laugh and sipped his drink. "Howie's old-school. My old man *went* to the old school but *wasn't* old-school."

For the first time, Ellery felt like he was getting accurate, maybe even unbiased information on Tristan Wallace and his clan. Now it made sense why Jack had wanted him to talk to Rowdy. It also cleared up the mystery of what someone like Jack had liked about someone like Rowdy Wallace. Jack was all about honesty and candor, and Rowdy seemed as direct as a bullet between the eyes.

"Nobody but Howie thinks my old man offed himself," Rowdy added.

"Okay, but why did he sail out alone that evening?"

"See, that's something I never understood. Why they tried to make so much of that. He used to take the boat out in the evening all the time. He liked night sailing. Especially when he wanted to clear his head."

"I see." Definitely a different perspective. "Why are you so sure Odette murdered him, though? She'd have had to have help, which would be risky—people talk—plus, it seems like plenty of others had motive."

"Hell yes, she had help. I'm not suggesting Odette went after him on jet skis. I've never seen anyone less coordinated. She hired someone. Of course. As for other people having motive? Did they really? Sure, the old man had enemies, but do you really kill someone over a lousy business deal?"

"People do." Though judging by the True Crime section at the Crow's Nest, not as often as they killed each other over love, lust, jealousy, oh, and fear. Fear was a major driver for violence.

Or were those simply the motives that made for better reading?

Rowdy shrugged. "Okay, maybe. I'll give you that. But do they do it in such a complicated way? Wouldn't they hire someone to run his car off a cliff or shoot him in a home invasion gone wrong?"

Probably. That's how Ellery would… Well, no. Ellery couldn't think of any circumstances that would drive him to murder.

"Yes, Van, Mason, and I are about to inherit a big chunk of change. We'd have inherited a lot more if the old man had divorced Odette before he kicked off."

That was a good point.

"What about Mr. King?"

Rowdy looked surprised. "Howie? Howie isn't the sensitive type. And from a practical standpoint, I don't see what he'd have to gain. He's already rich, and he has exactly the same job he always had and always would've had."

"Your father hadn't threatened to fire him or anything?"

"Fire *Howie*?" Rowdy laughed. "Oh, maybe he *threatened*, but never in a million years. For one thing, Howie knows where all the bodies are buried. For another, would you really fire the guy who helped make you filthy rich? The old man used to threaten to fire everyone including me, Mason, and Van. The only one he wouldn't *ever* have fired was Howie. And Howie knew it."

"Okay." Ellery considered the remaining possibilities.

Rowdy said suddenly, "Have we met? You look familiar."

Ellery blinked. "I just have one of those faces."

Rowdy grinned. "Uh, no, you really *don't*."

Ellery ignored that. "If your father was that difficult to get along with, wouldn't it have been easier, less risky for Odette, to go ahead and divorce him? They were married a long time. Wouldn't there have been a decent settlement?"

Rowdy said succinctly, "Prenup."

"Uh-oh."

"Exactly." Rowdy added, "And he *was* going to divorce her this time. Not because he thought she was having an affair. She did have a thing with the pool boy, but that had been a while back. I don't think it was anything like that, to be honest. I think he was tired of her. Bored. Ten years ago, she wasn't bad-looking, but she wasn't the nubile babe she'd been when he met her."

Nubile babe was definitely not a term Ellery would have applied to Odette.

"He said looking at her made him feel old."

Wow. King had it right. Not a nice man.

"Still," Ellery said. "Murder? It's complicated. And this one was more complicated than most."

"I see your dilemma," Rowdy said. "But if you think about it, there just isn't another viable suspect. She did it. The only question is how."

"Well, not the only question. Who did she get to help her?"

"Probably someone on the island." Rowdy suddenly put his glass down, staring at Ellery. "Holy— You're Noah Street!"

Ellery looked around guiltily, not because he didn't know who Rowdy was talking to, but because he was hoping no one in the pub heard that.

As though Ellery had denied it, Rowdy insisted, "Yes, you are. I'd know you anywhere."

"*Shhh.* Can you not?" Ellery pleaded.

"Oh my God. I saw every one of those *Happy Halloween! You're Dead!* movies. The last one where your old girlfriend comes back as a gargoyle and you have to save your new girlfriend from her and the three of you end up mud-wrestling in the graveyard."

Ellery made a pained sound.

"They are The Best movies in the world to watch drunk."

"Better to be drunk making them too."

Rowdy laughed. "Does Jack know?"

Ellery made another of those will-someone-put-me-out-of-my-misery? Sounds.

Rowdy laughed again and raised his empty glass to get Frankie's attention.

"This calls for another round! Let's drink to Noah Street. The Final Boy."

CHAPTER EIGHTEEN

None of which explained why Odette would pretend someone was trying to kill her.

Or, assuming Odette was telling the truth—and Ellery stubbornly persisted in believing she was— why anyone would want to kill Odette.

How did killing Odette serve anyone's purpose?

What was in Odette's will? Was there any way of finding out?

He was trying to think whether Jack might be able to access that information—and if there was any way to convince Jack to share it with him—when he reached the Crow's Nest.

The bell had a muted quality as he opened the door and cautiously stuck his head in.

A churchlike hush seemed to envelop the book-shop.

Uneasily, he studied the wide, airy room. Rupert, the costumed skeleton who served as the shop mascot, grinned in silent welcome.

Kingston was reshelving books. He nodded courteously and continued returning books to their rightful places. Nora was going over shipping invoices at the front desk. A few customers wandered around, probably looking for the restroom.

It all felt eerily normal.

Watson came to greet Ellery, and Ellery knelt to spend a few seconds saying hello.

"How was your meeting, dearie?" Nora asked politely.

Clearly space aliens had arrived while Ellery was out, and abducted his staff.

He said doubtfully, "Fine. Everything okay here?"

"Yes, indeed," Nora said.

As Ellery joined her at the sales desk, he noticed an arrangement of yellow roses and white daisy spray chrysanthemums in a small vase next to the raven paperweight. He nearly asked who they were for, but realized in time that the card had already been removed. The envelope was in the wastepaper basket, and Nora's cheeks were suspiciously pink.

Okay. Well, Ellery was not going to tamper with what appeared to be a successful, peaceful treaty.

"I'll be in my office. I have to make some phone calls," he told Nora.

"Very well, dearie."

Ellery turned away. Among other things, he was determined to finally corner the elusive Mr. Honeycutt, but the bell on the front door sounded again, and a very large man, dressed in black jeans and a black sweatshirt, entered the bookshop. He did not look like a reader, but as Ellery had learned over the past months, you couldn't judge a book by its cover.

The man's gaze dismissed Kingston, dismissed Nora, dismissed the nearest customer, and settled like a red-dot sight on Ellery.

"Ellery Page." His voice was low and raspy, like a comic book henchman. He didn't wait for Ellery to respond. "Mrs. Wallace wants to see you."

"Now?" Ellery glanced around in surprise. Everyone else in the bookshop looked equally surprised.

"That's what she says."

"Well, okay. I was just about to phone her."

Watson, normally delighted to meet everyone who crossed their threshold, cautiously approached the large man, sniffing suspiciously at his brown neoprene boots. Whatever he smelled on those slip-resistant outsoles had him somersaulting backward.

Watson picked himself up and began to bark.

Arf! Arf! Arf!

The man's face darkened, but Kingston sprinted over and scooped up Watson with an out-of-breath, "Now! None of that, pup!"

Watson wriggled indignantly, muttering under his breath and throwing out the occasional *Arf!*

"Tackle Shandy, I know your grandma!" Nora called in apparent warning.

Tackle grinned. "And she thinks you're an old busybody just like I do, Nora Sweeny!"

Nora's eyes narrowed with indignation. She opened her mouth to reply, but Ellery grabbed his jacket—it was cold on the water—and came around the desk. "Okay, time to go."

"I'm phoning Chief Carson right now," Nora announced, breezing past him as she headed into his office.

Tackle burst out laughing. "Do you think I'm kidnapping him? He works for the lady!" He held the door for Ellery, shaking his head. "What a bunch of nuts!"

It was the boots, really.

Or maybe Watson's reaction to the boots, because nearly every fisherman on the island stomped around in those Xtratuf Legacy Boots.

The boots *and* Tackle's unruly red hair, which grew in tufts (including out of his ears). But it was also the way Tackle watched him with those bright blue-gray eyes, as though he could hardly keep from laughing out loud at a joke that was on Ellery.

They weren't even halfway across the harbor before Ellery was one hundred percent sure Tackle was the one who'd broken into Captain's Seat and the Crow's Nest.

That was instinct, not evidence. Instinct based on the way Tackle kept looking at him and grinning that huge grin. Ellery suspected Tackle didn't even care whether Ellery had guessed he was the midnight intruder. He found that funny too.

Ellery…not so much. He wasn't afraid of Tackle, exactly, but the guy was an ex-felon and intimidating, no question. Ellery definitely didn't want to get on his bad side. At least, not while they were zipping across the water in the *Windsong*'s tender boat.

"So you're the one who found Vernon," Tackle shouted over the *pbpbpbpbbppbpbpbp* of the outboard and the wash of sea spray.

Why did everyone insist Ellery was the one who'd found the body in Buccaneer's Bay? Jack had been there too. Ellery would never have been on the *Roussillon* if not for Jack.

"Did I? I didn't know the body had been identified yet," Ellery yelled back.

Tackle shrugged. "That's what everyone says."

True enough. "What do you say?"

"Me?" Tackle's bushy red brows rose in surprise. "How would I know? I wasn't even born then."

That was true. Tackle was probably in his forties. Way too young to have any involvement in Vernon's disappearance or death.

"Does the rest of your family think it's Vernon in that diving suit?"

Tackle said cagily, "Not in that suit now, is he?"

"No."

"No. You'd have to ask them." Tackle's smile was less friendly that time.

Ellery astonished himself by calling, "I'd rather ask you what you were searching for in my house and my shop."

That startled Tackle so much, his hand swerved on the tiller, and the little boat veered sharply, dousing them with cold, salty spray, before Tackle corrected course. He wasn't alarmed, though. He burst out laughing.

"Prove it was me."

"I wish I could."

Tackle grinned, shook his head. "You can't. 'Cuz I don't know what you're talking about." He had the gall to wink at Ellery.

Ellery said, "What do you think Vernon was doing out there?"

Tackle stopped grinning. "Everyone knows Vernon spent all his time looking for the *Blood Red Rose*'s treasure. He was crazy for those old pirate legends."

"Sure, but what would he have been doing on the *Roussillon*?"

Tackle frowned. "No idea." He seemed genuinely mystified.

By then, they had reached Mrs. Wallace's yacht. Ellery was half expecting Tackle to whisper some threat to keep his mouth shut, but in fact, he was silent and polite as he helped Ellery out of the tender and led the way up the sundeck, where Mrs. Wallace and Mr. King were once again drinking champagne and catching some rays.

The mini wolf pack greeted Ellery with snarls of outrage at his daring to return to their den. Mrs.

Wallace shushed them half-heartedly, removing her oversize sunglasses to glare at Ellery.

"What have you been doing all this time? I said I wanted progress reports twice a day!"

Mr. King, shiny with suntan oil and perspiration, looked apologetic and vaguely guilty. "I meant to touch base with you earlier, Mr. Page. I'm sorry."

Mrs. Wallace frowned. "Why are you apologizing, Howard? It's *not* your fault. I told Mr. Page what I wanted. Apparently, he thinks I paid him all that money because I enjoy looking at his pretty face."

Where had she learned her lines? From her famously rude husband?

Ellery said politely, "No. But I thought you might prefer that I have something to report before we met again."

"Twice. A. Day," Mrs. Wallace snapped.

"Okay. Twice a day." As soon as he earned out that advance, he was handing in his notice. Unless she was arrested first. After his meeting with Colby, that was starting to seem like a possibility. Especially now that Jack was on her tail.

"Well? What have you found out?"

Not enough. That was for sure.

"I talked to Vanessa, Mason, and Colby." He glanced at Mr. King. "By the way, who's Bailey?"

"She was Colby's fiancée."

Mrs. Wallace, predictably, commented, "*Horrible* girl."

Ellery managed to control his exasperation. "Okay, well, however horrible they all are, they do seem genuinely convinced that you murdered your husband."

Surprisingly, that seemed to shock her. "No, they don't. They just want the money." She turned to Mr. King as if for reassurance.

"Can they produce any kind of alibi, either singly or together?" King demanded crisply.

Ellery didn't bother to hide his puzzlement. "Neither you nor Mrs. Wallace are able to pinpoint when you think these attempts took place, so how are they going to be able to provide alibis?"

"The answer is no," King informed him.

Mrs. Wallace nodded approvingly.

"I mean, I guess the police could ask them to try to reconstruct their movements over the past months. I can't. I don't have that authority."

"So far, you're not a lot of help," Mrs. Wallace said.

So true. But having gone this far, Ellery was determined to hang on to that advance. He said, "It's still early in my investigation. I expect to have more information—" He nearly lost his balance as the yacht rocked sideways as though shoved by a giant hand. From across the harbor, he caught a flash of red light and then—

BOOM!

The blast was deafening. The ocean seemed to slosh back and forth like water in a bowl. Bits of wood, fiberglass, and burning canvas began to rain down on the deck of the *Windsong*.

What the hell?

Ears ringing, heart pounding, Ellery ducked down, sheltering beneath the awning over the sundeck, covering his mouth and nose in the crook of his arm. Even so, the air had an acrid, burnt taste to it.

Had that been a *bomb*? Was that possible?

If so, it wasn't on the *Windsong*. That was the good news.

The bad news…

Sirens were going off in the village, the sound echoing across the water. Alarm bells filled the smoky air. People were screaming from the other boats. The little white dogs were going crazy, howling over and over. Ellery looked across at his companions.

"J-Jesus Christ!" Mr. King, still sitting in his lounge chair, looked more stupefied than anything.

Had he not believed the threats against her were real?

But then, that was the thing. Mrs. Wallace was unharmed.

Ellery stared, watching Tackle helping her to her feet. Other than having lost her sunglasses and having blackened bits in her hair, Ellery's employer seemed okay. In fact, she pushed Tackle aside and cautiously picked her way through the burning debris to the side of the boat. Staring across the harbor at the flaming fireball of what had once been a yacht, she gave a weird laugh.

She turned to Mr. King and cried, "That's the *Wet Dreams*. Those morons blew up Mason!"

CHAPTER NINETEEN

Jane Smith swallowed the last of her rum punch and said in slightly slurred tones, "At leasht no one was injured in the blasht, so that's good news."

At Ellery's look of disbelief, Jane blushed. She said quickly, "No one from the village, I mean. None of *us*."

"Mason Wallace was killed," Ellery said. He was still deeply shocked.

"Right. That's terrible. But he *was* building a bomb to kill hish stepmother."

Ellery didn't reply, but yes, three days following the fatal blast aboard the *Wet Dreams*, the Rhode Island State Bomb Squad (or, as it was officially known, the Technical Services Unit of the Law Enforcement Bureau of the Office of the State Fire Marshal) had determined that Mason Wallace—head of the Sustainable Technologies division of Wallace Industries *and* possessing a degree in Chemical Engineering——had died while constructing an explosive device aboard his yacht.

Ellery, stricken to realize he'd never even considered looking into the educational and professional background of any of his prime suspects, had vowed to hang up his deerstalker for good. Not that knowing Mason's background would have changed much. No previous attempts had been made to blow up Odette Wallace, but it just demonstrated the gaps in Ellery's investigation.

As much as he enjoyed mysteries, he really wasn't any good at solving them. Unfortunately, Mrs. Wallace agreed and was demanding a full refund.

Unsurprising, then, that Ellery was not in much of a party mood that Saturday as he stood with Talia and George in the crowded striped tent housing the celebration of the 100th anniversary of Pirate's Cove's Historical Society.

Jane departed in hot pursuit of a tray of shrimp puffs, and Talia murmured, "*What* a weirdo. Tell me she's not a dear friend!"

"I don't think she's used to drinking," Ellery said.

Talia held up her plastic punch cup. "Can you call this drinking?"

George checked his watch and said reluctantly, "I was hoping we'd see Jack before we left, but we should probably think about heading over to the ferry."

"*Boo,*" Talia replied. She looked at Ellery and pulled an exaggerated sad face. But in fact, her eyes were way too bright. "I can't believe the week is already over."

"Me neither." He was embarrassed at how choky his voice got. He was really, really going to miss them. "Let me give Jack a call and see if he can get away."

That was unlikely. Jack had his hands full with the Fire Marshal's investigation as well as the ongoing inquiry into the body at Buccaneer's Bay homicide. Beyond verifying that the other was safe—which had included a nearly bone-cracking but all-too-brief hug——Ellery had barely seen Jack since the day of the explosion.

That was how it went when your boyfriend was the chief of police. If Ellery didn't like it, now would be the time to figure that out.

"No, don't bother him," George said. "He'd be here if he could."

That was true, but what did it say that in the course of a week George had come to know Jack that well?

"I'll walk over with you," Ellery began but was interrupted by a tearful Nora, who threw her arms around him and hugged him with all her might.

"I can't believe you did that," she sniffed when she raised her head. "You're just the dearest, *dearest* boy."

Ellery laughed and hugged her back. It was actually the third time Nora had done this following his presentation that morning. It had taken some doing, but he had finally managed to pin down Mr. Honeycutt and arrange to lease the bottom level of Skull House to the Pirate's Cove Historical Society for the grand total of fifty dollar a month for the next fifty years.

"Just don't pay me back by resigning to go work full-time at Skull House."

"*Never!*" Nora cried. "Never in a million years." She turned once again to tell Talia and George what a wonderful son they had, and Ellery stepped back—colliding with a very solid someone.

"Sorry!" he apologized to a slightly glassy-eyed Cap Murphy.

"Ellery!" Cap greeted him on a gust of rum punch. "That was a great thing you did for this village. Eudora would be proud of you. You're a true Page. You're a Page true and true." Cap laughed heartily at his own joke.

Ellery said gravely, "Thank you, Cap."

"It's the whole struth and nothing but the struth." Cap peered at him with bleary eyes. "Did you see Sue?"

Sue Lewis, owner and editor-in-chief of the *Scuttlebutt Weekly*, was no pal of Ellery's. In fact, she was kind of his archenemy, not that anyone over the age of ten should have an archenemy.

"Is Sue here?" Ellery glanced around apprehensively. He hadn't seen Sue since she'd—as Nora put it—fallen afoul of the law. Which had apparently amounted to a slap on the wrist and a few weeks of community service.

"Somewhere," Cap said cheerfully. "She wants to interview you for the paper."

"Hahahaha," Ellery said.

"No, but I'm serious."

"So am I!"

"Hey!" Cap said as though he had only just spotted Ellery. "*Hey.*"

Ellery looked to either side. Maybe Cap was seeing double Ellerys? It seemed likely.

"I just remembered. Your collection bag. Did you get it?"

"My what?"

"I dropped it off with that kid who used to work for you. The one who was in the play. The mayor's kid."

"I..." *Have no idea what you're talking about,* was what Ellery was going to say, but he was interrupted by Talia, who said into his ear, "Baby, George wants to leave for the ferry."

He nodded. "I'm right behind you."

Talia squeezed his arm, said goodbye to the little circle of admirers who had gathered around her, and she and George began to edge toward the tent entrance.

Ellery turned back to Cap, who said, "Your collection bag. You left it on the boat that day. The day we found...you know. *The suit.*"

A little alarm bell seemed to go off inside Ellery's head.

"I didn't have a collection bag that day."

"Sure you did," Cap said. He held his hands up. "Yea big. You left it on the deck in all the excitement."

"Jack carried a collection bag. Is that what you're thinking of?"

"It wasn't Jack's bag. It was older than that. Jack's equipment is all top-of-the-line."

True that. So was it possible…?

Ellery's pulse quickened with excitement. "You said you gave the bag to Felix?"

"That's right. I dropped it off with him at the bookstore on my way home."

"Hey, can you excuse me for a minute?"

Cap waved him off.

Ellery stepped away, dug his cell phone out, and called Felix.

The call went straight to message, which made sense. What kid spent his first weekend in college sitting in his dorm, waiting for the phone to ring?

But didn't these kids keep their phones glued to their hands?

He tried again. Again, the call went to message.

Ellery hunted through his contacts for Libby's phone number. That call too went straight to message.

Argh.

Okay, well, it's not like it was an *emergency.* Sure, this could maybe answer one mystery, but would it really change the outcome of…anything?

Probably not, but he still *really* wanted to know.

He looked around the crowded tent for a possible solution, realized his parents had left.

Yikes.

He started after them but was stopped by an urgent, "Ellery?"

He turned. Robert Mane, looking startlingly handsome in jeans and a black skull-and-crossbones T-shirt, beamed at him. "Hi? Have your parents left yet? I wanted to say goodbye."

"Yeah, they just took off."

Robert looked disappointed. "That's a shame. I was hoping to—"

"I'll let them know," Ellery threw over his shoulder, making for the tent entrance.

He navigated his way through the throng of people like a quarterback scrambling through the defense, and sped after his parents.

The air outside the tent was warm and breezy. Gulls swooped overhead, crying out lazily. Ellery shielded his eyes from the glare off the water and spotted Talia and George strolling along several yards down the boardwalk.

He paused to try phoning Jack, fully expecting it to go straight to message there too, but Jack answered, surprising him.

"Hey, how's the party?"

"Big success. Nora got a huge turnout. I think everyone in the village is here."

"Great. Sorry to miss it. When are your parents leaving for the ferry?"

"We're walking over now."

"*Now?*" Jack sounded startled. "Okay, well, I think I can get away for a few minutes."

Ellery's heart warmed. He knew exactly how busy and harassed Jack was right now, so just the offer meant a lot. However, he had more important things on his mind.

"No, no. Don't worry about it. They understand. Jack, I wanted to—"

Jack said firmly, "No way. I can take the time to say goodbye."

"Jack, I just talked to Cap Murphy, and he says he left a collection bag at the Crow's Nest. Did you grab your collection bag that day we found the body in the diving suit?"

Jack said in a very different tone, "I brought all my gear home that day."

"I didn't have a collection bag."

Jack, as usual, saw exactly where Ellery was headed. He swore. "The diver's collection bag must have been overlooked somehow."

"That's what I'm thinking too."

"What happened to the bag?"

"Cap says he left it with Felix, but I didn't see it anywhere in the shop. I'm afraid—"

"Have you talked to Felix?"

"I left a message. I think that collection bag must have been what the intruder was after at the Crow's Nest and Captain's Seat."

Jack made a sound that fell somewhere between a groan and a growl. "What do you think was in the bag?"

"I guess it could be anything from mussels to..." The idea that came to Ellery took his breath away.

Jack prodded, "To?"

"Treasure?"

"Are you kidding?"

"Sort of? What about a map? Or no. Maybe some proof the *Blood Red Rose* exists?"

Jack was silent.

"Gold doubloons?" Ellery pressed. "Whatever was in that bag had some weight. It clinked."

"*Clinked.*" Jack's tone was skeptical.

"I barely noticed at the time, but yeah. I remember the *chink-chink* of something metallic." Ellery added guiltily, "I think I might have been the one who un-clipped the bag from the suit."

"So what exactly are you saying?"

"According to several people, Vernon Shandy spent all his free time hunting for the wreck of the *Blood Red Rose.*"

"You think Vernon Shandy found the *Blood Red Rose*?" Jack's tone was thoughtful rather than excited.

"That, I can't say, but I do think this is pretty good proof that the body we found belonged to Vernon Shandy. What he would have been doing in an old div-ing suit or even on the *Roussillon*, I don't know, but—"

Jack cut in with a brusque, "The skeleton we found doesn't belong to Vernon Shandy."

"But—"

"I just got the ME's report. Our victim was a middle-aged male, approximately five feet tall. Shandy was thirty-two years old and over six feet tall. The body in the diving suit was not Shandy's."

"Then…"

Jack said nothing.

And just like that, the puzzle pieces began to click into place.

"Tristan Wallace," Ellery said. "But I don't understand. How did Wallace get into Vernon's diving suit?"

"First of all, we don't know that diving suit belonged to Vernon. In fact, it's pretty unlikely."

"Okay, maybe not Vernon, but there's a good chance it belonged to the Shandys."

"Maybe. It's far from con-"

"Okay, just hear me out." Ellery was following his own thoughts. "Ten years ago, the Historical Society was closing up shop. All their exhibits went into a warehouse. Maybe Mason noticed and decided to grab one of the exhibits to use as a hiding place for his father's body. Because the idea was that if the body could never be found, no one could be prosecuted. He just had to wait ten years until the trust terminated."

No comment from Jack.

"But I still don't understand why Mason wanted to kill his father." Ellery stared out at the wide blue, and nearly empty, harbor. Race Week had come to an abrupt and unpleasant end with Mason's death.

Still nothing from Jack.

"I don't know why he didn't notice there was something in the collection bag, but he would have been in a desperate hurry and maybe he didn't notice or care if there was something in there."

Jack said, "Taking the suit might have been impulse. It's possible Wallace's murder wasn't completely premeditated."

Not *completely* premeditated? Wasn't that like being sort of pregnant?

Ellery said, "What doesn't make sense is why Mason identified that body found in Newport as his father."

"Is that what happened?" Jack asked.

"Isn't it?"

Boom. The truth was as obvious and startling as a homemade bomb exploding on a summer's day.

"No, it isn't." Ellery answered his own question. "*That's* why Mason had to die. And also because—since Wallace's body was discovered and the case was being reopened—someone needed to be found guilty of Wallace's murder. Someone had to be the fall guy."

"I think Mason's days were numbered anyway, but yeah. Once that body was found, Mason had to go—and *before* he figured out, he'd wrongly identified the drowning victim in Newport."."

"Which leaves… Wait. *Howard?*"

"King was also present when that John Doe was incorrectly identified as Tristan Wallace."

"But why…"

"I'm not sure if he somehow coerced Mason into falsely identifying the body or if Mason just wasn't paying close enough attention, but once the body in the diving suit was discovered, Mason became a liability for Howard King. King needed to get rid of him fast, and he also needed someone to blame Wallace's murder on. Blowing up Mason solved two problems with one bomb. The problem for King is that we knew right away Mason had been murdered."

"You did?" Ellery grimaced. That was something Jack hadn't shared with him. Granted, he'd barely talked to Jack since Wednesday. They certainly hadn't had any time alone together. Would Jack have confided in him, if they'd been together?

"Yep. According to the Fire Marshal, someone with Mason's background would never have resorted to building such a crude and dangerous device. It would have been suicide. It's probable he was already dead before the bomb went off."

Luckily for Bailey, she had been off shopping in the village. Or had that been luck? Was Bailey's escape a bit of chivalry on the part of *old-school* Howard King?

Ellery thought of Howard, slick with oil and sweat, sitting in the lounge chair, waiting for that bomb to go off—and his flabbergasted expression when the blast turned out to be so much larger than he'd expected.

"But I still don't understand why someone like King would do that. What did he have to gain?"

"Mrs. Wallace." Jack added, "King has a soft spot for the ladies, and Mrs. Wallace was a very rich and very lonely lady."

"But King was engaged to someone else back then."

"He didn't marry her, did he?"

"No, I guess not." Ellery watched the figures of his parents growing smaller in the distance. He started walking, then picked up the pace. "He had to have help. He couldn't've hid the body on his own."

"He's got his own yacht. He dives. He could have done it alone, but it seems more likely he had help."

"So there never was any actual murder plot against Odette?"

"No. You said it yourself: those attempts were so broad, they were almost farcical. She was never in actual danger. The intent was to strengthen her position and throw more suspicion on Mason."

"So she was she involved in killing her husband?"

He was surprised when Jack hesitated. "We won't know until we question her."

"Wow. That's... Well, congratulations on solving the case."

Jack laughed. "Don't sound so disheartened. I was literally only two hours ahead of you, and I have all the resources of law enforcement."

"Now you're just trying to make me feel better."

"Of course. The warrant for King's arrest is being drawn up now. I'll meet you down at the ferry in ten minutes."

Ellery's heart lightened. He said, "You know, you really don't have to."

"I know." Ellery could hear the smile in Jack's voice, and he smiled too. "See you then," Jack said.

Ellery began to run.

EPILOGUE

"**Y**ou know, if you solved *all* the mysteries in this village before me, I'd have to hand in my badge." Jack's fingers lightly combed through Ellery's hair.

Ellery's smile was rueful. "I know. It's not a competition."

Jack said firmly, "No. It's not."

Watson, his head pillowed on Ellery's foot, was snoring, and Ellery, his head pillowed on Jack's chest, started laughing.

"Why is that so funny?" Ellery wondered.

Jack was grinning. "All that sound coming out of that little body?"

No lie, there was *a lot* of sound coming out of that furry black body. Watson's snores were loud enough to drown out the summer night sounds of crickets and the breeze stirring the open draperies.

"Maybe that's it."

Ellery said thoughtfully, "I wonder what *did* happen to Vernon Shandy?"

"Probably in Canada right now, bouncing a little gang of felons on his knee."

Ellery snorted.

Jack asked curiously, "What did your mom whisper to you that got you all choked up?"

Ellery thought back to the moment before his mom had started up the gangplank. "Oh." He smiled.

"This one's a keeper," Talia had whispered, her eyes very bright. Anyone who had watched Jack in action over the past few days as he worked tirelessly to ensure the safety and welfare of everyone on the island, would have had to agree.

Jack lightly tickled Ellery's ribs. "*Oh* what?"

Ellery chuckled but didn't reply.

"Okay," Jack said lightly. "Keep your secrets."

Ellery tilted his face up. "No secrets. She said you're a keeper."

Jack—what Ellery could see of him at that angle—turned red.

He said gruffly, "That was nice of her. She's a nice lady."

"Yeah. She is."

They were quiet for a time, just enjoying finally being alone together again.

But then Jack sighed. "We weren't able to get anything useful off your letter."

"Letter?" Ellery said blankly. "Oh, right. *That* letter." So much had happened in the past week, he'd *almost* forgotten about his poison-pen pal.

Jack said comfortingly, "Don't worry. We'll get them next time."

Ugh. Next time. Yes, there would surely be a next time.

Ellery said with fake confidence, "I know. The security cameras will help." A brand-new security system, complete with cameras, was to be installed first thing Monday morning at the Crow's Nest.

Jack kissed his ear. "They will. Thank you for getting that taken care of."

Ellery gave Jack the side-eye—well, it was kind of an upside-down eye—and said, "How do you like the new and improved, safety-conscious me?"

"I like him."

Is he a keeper? But of course, Ellery didn't ask.

"Anyway, I'm not nearly as worried as I was when I thought my stalker was the one breaking into Captain's Seat and the Crow's Nest."

"Oh yeah, having convicted felons coming and going at will is *much* better," Jack agreed.

Ellery sighed. "Tackle found what he was after, so I don't think there'll be much coming and going from the Shandys."

Felix had called Ellery back that evening and, when he finally recollected Cap dropping off the collection bag, admitted he'd left it on one of the office storage shelves.

"Did you look inside?" Ellery had asked.

No, Felix had not looked inside because he was already late for picking Libby up for their going-away party.

Ellery sighed again.

"Still thinking of your lost pirate's treasure?"

Ellery reached up, hand clawed toward the ceiling, crying in his best Shakespearean actor voice, "It could have been mine! *All mine!*"

He couldn't help thinking, though, that whoever had first hidden the suit in the warehouse had to have known what was in the collection bag. Did that mean the point of hiding the suit had been to conceal whatever was in that bag?

Conceal what from whom?

They'd probably never know.

Jack laughed, and Ellery's head bumped up and down. "You're a nut, Page. You know that?"

Ellery glanced up at Captain Horatio Page. "It runs in the family."

"I bet it does. So do you think your mom's okay with your choices?"

"I'm not sure I like the segue from nuts to my mom."

Jack made a sound of amusement. He said, "I think it's hard not to dream a future for your kids."

Ellery was quiet, thinking of Jack's dreams for a baby that was never born. But Jack was thinking along other lines because he said ruefully, "My dad was pretty disappointed when I told him I was going into the police academy. Instead, my brother-in-law became my dad's construction business partner."

"Rowdy said he couldn't believe it when you told him you were becoming a police officer."

"You and Rowdy talked about me?" Jack didn't sound happy about that.

"That was the extent of it. Why *did* you become a police officer?"

Jack's mouth quirked. "The usual. I hated sleeping, wanted to work holidays, love lots of stress and being underpaid."

"So it was a dream come true."

"Yep."

Ellery said, "The thing is, my mom always wanted to be an actor, but her parents thought it was a really bad idea. They insisted she get a good education, so she trained to be a teacher. But even after she was hired to teach, she kept going on auditions and getting parts, and eventually she met my dad, and they married, and she quit teaching and really concentrated on her acting. She's really good."

"I believe it."

"She was building a career for herself, but then my dad died, and, because of me, she felt she needed more stability, more financial security, so she went back to teaching."

Jack, as usual, was able to sift through the chaff and get straight to the wheat. "You're saying, your acting career was your mother's dream, not yours."

"Well, I don't know if that's totally true. I mean, I had a blast doing those first *Happy Halloween! You're Dead!* movies. And the money was ridiculously good. But the films got worse and worse, and it stopped being fun. I was too old to keep playing the Final Boy in a horror franchise, and I wasn't getting offered—wasn't good enough, frankly—for better parts." Ellery shrugged. "I was at a dead end when I inherited all this."

Jack said, "Hollywood's loss is Pirate's Cove's gain."

Ellery chuckled.

"I have a confession. I watched the first two *Happy Halloween!* movies last night."

Ellery rolled over (to Watson's displeasure) so that they were face-to-face. "*Two?* You must have a high pain threshold."

"No. They're..."

"Bad."

"I wouldn't say that."

Ellery grinned. "Well, no, because you want to sleep with me."

"The plot is better in the first movie. But you're better in the second. You seemed genuinely frightened."

"I'd read the reviews of the first film."

Jack laughed. He said, "Hey, I have something for you."

Ellery wiggled his eyebrows, and Jack said, "Hold that thought."

He rose, retrieved his jeans from the wooden trunk at the foot of the bed, dug through his pockets, and tossed something small and shiny to Ellery.

Ellery caught it, opened his hand, and considered the ordinary brass key. "What's this for?"

"This is for those nights you don't feel like driving back here."

"Really? That's..." Jack looked a little self-conscious climbing back into bed, so Ellery settled for a casual, "Thanks."

"You're welcome." Jack stretched his arm in invitation, and Ellery settled his head once more on Jack's shoulder.

Watson regarded them for a long moment, then tucked his head beneath his tail, sighed, and closed his eyes.

AUTHOR'S NOTE

Dear Reader,

Welcome once again to Pirate's Cove, where sinister shadows lurk behind every corner of our cute, quaint village. So many murders! Such a little police force! And we're only getting started. ;-)

These stories are set on fictional Buck Island. The character of Watson is based on my own adopted pup Spenser (formerly known as Watson).

Thank you as ever to dear, dear Keren. Thank you to Kevin. Thank you to Emily-Bemily.

Thank YOU, dear readers. I could not make this voyage without you.

LAMENT AT
LOON LANDING

SECRETS AND SCRABBLE BOOK SIX

FAKES, FOLK MUSIC, AND GHOST FIRES

When legendary folk singer Lara Fairplay agrees to make her comeback appearance at Pirate's Cove's annual maritime music festival, everyone in the quaint seaside village is delighted, including mystery bookstore owner and sometimes amateur sleuth, Ellery Page.

Lara is scheduled to perform a recently discovered piece of music attributed to "the father of American music," Stephen Foster.

Several mysterious accidents later, Ellery is less delighted, especially when it becomes clear to him that someone plans to silence the celebrity songbird forever.

ABOUT THE AUTHOR

Author of over sixty titles of classic Male/Male fiction featuring twisty mystery, kickass adventure, and unapologetic man-on-man romance, JOSH LANYON'S work has been translated into twelve languages. Her FBI thriller *Fair Game* was the first Male/Male title to be published by Harlequin Mondadori, then the largest romance publisher in Italy. *Stranger on the Shore* (Harper Collins Italia) was the first M/M title to be published in print. In 2016 *Fatal Shadows* placed #5 in Japan's annual Boy Love novel list (the first and only title by a foreign author to place on the list). The Adrien English series was awarded the All Time Favorite Couple by the Goodreads M/M Romance Group. In 2019, *Fatal Shadows* became the first LGBTQ mobile game created by *Moments: Choose Your Story.*

She is an Eppie Award winner, a four-time Lambda Literary Award finalist (twice for Gay Mystery), an Edgar nominee, and the first ever recipient of the Goodreads All Time Favorite M/M Author award.

Josh is married and lives in Southern California.

Find other Josh Lanyon titles at www.joshlanyon.com, and follow Josh on Twitter, Facebook, Goodreads, Instagram and Tumblr.

For extras and exclusives, join Josh on Patreon.

ALSO BY JOSH LANYON

NOVELS

The ADRIEN ENGLISH Mysteries
Fatal Shadows • A Dangerous Thing • The Hell You Say
Death of a Pirate King • The Dark Tide
Stranger Things Have Happened • So This is Christmas •

The HOLMES & MORIARITY Mysteries
Somebody Killed His Editor • All She Wrote
The Boy with the Painful Tattoo • In Other Words...Murder

The ALL'S FAIR Series
Fair Game • Fair Play • Fair Chance

The ART OF MURDER Series
The Mermaid Murders •The Monet Murders
The Magician Murders • The Monuments Men Murders

BEDKNOBS AND BROOMSTICKS
Mainly by Moonlight • I Buried a Witch
Bell, Book and Scandal

The SECRETS AND SCRABBLE Series
Murder at Pirate's Cove • Secret at Skull House
Mystery at the Masquerade • Scandal at the Salty Dog
Body at Buccaneer's Bay

OTHER NOVELS

This Rough Magic • The Ghost Wore Yellow Socks
Mexican Heat (with Laura Baumbach) • Strange Fortune
Come Unto These Yellow Sands • Stranger on the Shore
Winter Kill • Jefferson Blythe, Esquire
Murder in Pastel • The Curse of the Blue Scarab
The Ghost Had an Early Check-out
Murder Takes the High Road • Séance on a Summer's Night

NOVELLAS

The DANGEROUS GROUND Series

Dangerous Ground • Old Poison • Blood Heat
Dead Run • Kick Start • Blind Side

OTHER NOVELLAS

Cards on the Table • The Dark Farewell • The Dark Horse
The Darkling Thrush • The Dickens with Love
I Spy Something Bloody • I Spy Something Wicked
I Spy Something Christmas • In a Dark Wood
The Parting Glass • Snowball in Hell • Mummy Dearest
Don't Look Back • A Ghost of a Chance
Lovers and Other Strangers • Out of the Blue
A Vintage Affair • Lone Star (in Men Under the Mistletoe)
Green Glass Beads (in Irregulars) • Blood Red Butterfly
Everything I Know • Baby, It's Cold (in Comfort and Joy)
A Case of Christmas • Murder Between the Pages
Slay Ride • Stranger in the House

SHORT STORIES

A Limited Engagement • The French Have a Word for It
In Sunshine or In Shadow • Until We Meet Once More
Icecapade (in His for the Holidays) • Perfect Day
Heart Trouble • Other People's Weddings (Petit Mort)
Slings and Arrows (Petit Mort)
Sort of Stranger Than Fiction (Petit Mort)
Critic's Choice (Petit Mort) • Just Desserts (Petit Mort)
In Plain Sight • Wedding Favors • Wizard's Moon
Fade to Black • Night Watch • Plenty of Fish
Halloween is Murder • The Boy Next Door
Requiem for Mr. Busybody

COLLECTIONS

Short Stories (Vol. 1) • Sweet Spot (the Petit Morts)
Merry Christmas, Darling (Holiday Codas)
Christmas Waltz (Holiday Codas 2) • I Spy...Three Novellas
Dangerous Ground The Complete Series
Dark Horse, White Knight (Two Novellas)
The Adrien English Mysteries Box Set
The Adrien English Mysteries Box Set 2
Male/Male Mystery & Suspense Box Set
Partners in Crime (Three Classic Gay Mystery Novels)
All's Fair Complete Collection
Shadows Left Behind: An Historical Mysteries Box Set